Kernels

Stories of People With a Softer Core

Ajay Gupte

INDIA • SINGAPORE • MALAYSIA

ISBN 979-8-89186-961-5

Index

(Dis)Honor

"ICE?" ASKED JAVED. "YES, a couple of pieces," replied Samar. Javed picked up two glasses from his bar, poured whiskey in both of them, and added a few pieces of ice. He then walked up to Samar and handed over a glass to him. They both started sipping their drinks. There was a pin-drop silence – it was a sprawling living room of a huge bungalow right in the middle of bustling Gurgaon. The room was very well made by a skilled interior designer to give it the look of an old-time 'haveli.' Finely designed heritage furniture added glamor and a prestigious look.

The two continued to sip their drinks. Halfway through, Javed asked, "Are you happy now?" Samar looked at Javed, then stared at his half-filled glass. He picked up the glass and gulped the remaining drink in one breath and banged the glass on the teapoy. There was an uncomfortable calm in the room. After a few minutes, Javed picked up the glasses again and refilled them with some more drink.

The two friends, Javed and Samar, had met after a long gap of almost thirty years. During this period, a lot had changed – their social status, their personal priorities, their attitude, and obviously the way they looked. But it took just a fraction of a second for both to recognize one another when they bumped into each other in a busy mall in Gurgaon. A busy Saturday evening ensured that the mall was bustling with a crowd, but the two guys were frozen for a few seconds staring at each other. Realizing that this wasn't the right place, Javed asked Samar if he was okay to accompany him to his bungalow nearby, and Samar agreed instantly. They drove a few minutes to reach a calm locality and finally reached Javed's bungalow. Javed's family had gone to the other city for a wedding, so there was dead silence in the house.

The two had met after thirty years, so there was a lot to talk about, but they just didn't want to begin, because they just didn't want to remember the incident thirty years back that made them part ways! But one had to start, so Samar asked, "You seem to have done really well, what do you do?" Javed smiled and acknowledged. He now owned a factory about fifty kilometers away and also had a plush office in Gurgaon. His factory now employed more than a thousand workers, and he was really doing well in business. "And you?" Javed asked. Samar smiled and said he was now the Mukhia of the four villages around Kund Chauraha. Both smiled at each other and sipped their whiskey.

Kund Chauraha – a junction in the interiors of Haryana was the place where it all began and where it all ended. The chauraha was a junction of two roads and a point where four small villages met. Each village hardly had a population of about fifty families but had vast open fields. Small as the villages were, everyone knew each other. Except for a few odd quarrels, it was largely a peaceful hamlet. Almost everyone in the village was engaged in farming. It was a rich fertile land, and the hardworking farmers did well for themselves. Days would start early in the village with men heading to farms for work, and the women would get busy with their daily chores. Children were pretty much left to themselves. The four villages shared a common government school which was a couple of miles from the chauraha. Children would generally meet their friends at the chauraha and then walk up to the school in groups. The elders would meet at the chauraha in the evening and spend time chatting and sipping tea.

Samar belonged to Sarang village. His father owned a huge farm, and he employed many laborers on his farms. He belonged to the influential zamindar community, and the family was well respected in the area. Samar was the elder of the two siblings. His younger sister Seema was a pampered child. The siblings gelled very well, and Samar was always protective of his sister. His father was the Mukhia of the four villages, and hence the family had an influence in the region. Samar's father had a big influence on his upbringing, and he was visibly groomed as an heir to the legacy. His father was strict and disciplined but at the same time, he took good care of the needs of the four villages. The fields in the area never had a scarcity of water, and the villages were assured of seeds and fertilizers on a timely manner. The villagers knew that they could reach out to their Mukhia even at the dead hour of the night in case of any problem.

Javed belonged to the neighboring Jamkhi village. Like Sarang, it was a small village close to the chauraha, on the other side. However, Jamkhi was visibly different from Sarang. The majority of the villagers belonged to the Muslim community. Many of them were farm laborers who normally picked up day jobs in the nearby farms to support their families. The villagers were less well-off compared to the other three villages in the area. Houses were small, and very few villagers owned farmlands. Like many, Javed's father was a poor farm laborer, but he worked hard to ensure a fulfilling life for his family of four.

Javed and his younger brother loved to go to school and study hard. Every morning, they would meet Samar at the chauraha, and then the trio walked up to the school. As if it was a routine, Samar and Javed met at the chauraha along with a few others, and then the group headed to the school. They would return as a group, and of course, the mood while returning from school was very jovial and happy. It would take more time to return as they would often wander in the fields or spend time playing around some trees. In the group, Javed was the most studious boy who really wanted to do something for his family. He could see his father's struggle and wanted to change the way they lived. Samar, on the other hand, was less interested in studies. He wasn't worried about the future, as he was destined to inherit vast stretches of lands.

Life seemed to be going at its own pace in these small villages. The villagers worked hard but never left a chance to enjoy themselves. Be it a festival or a marriage, almost all the families would assemble in a common place and enjoy every moment. The villages were a blend of people from different communities, religions, and social statuses. However, these differences were restricted to areas of faith and family. Friendships would always cut across all the lines, and for generations, they have all lived together. It looked like the perfect cinema story of peace and prosperity.

As days passed by, Samar and Javed completed their school studies. Samar started going to the nearby college a few kilometers from the chauraha. Javed, on the other hand, had to drop off. It seemed difficult for him to continue his studies given the financial condition of the family. In fact, Samar's father personally visited Javed and his family to offer financial help so that Javed could continue his studies, but Javed's father politely declined. So the two friends now had a different routine. Each morning, Samar would head to the college, and Javed to the nearby farm for working in the fields. However, the friends never missed a day meeting at the chauraha and spending their evenings together.

And then came the fateful morning that everyone in the village wants to forget for life. Seema, Samar's sister and daughter of the Mukhia of the villages went missing, and the entire village was out to look for her. Almost everyone in the village joined the teams to search for her. They searched the fields, the temple, the nearby stream, and every possible place, but no luck. Soon the news spread that a guy from Jamkhi village had also been missing since last night.

The environment in the villages changed within a minute. Tempers soared high, and everyone was furious. The fuel to the fire was the fact that the guy belonged to the other faith.

The villages had an unsaid rule. In general, they all were good friends and would jump to help one another, but marriages were strictly within the same community and religion. All these years, nobody had dared to cross this line. People now sensed that the most dreaded thing has happened. There was a very fragile peace in the morning, and by noon, it was clear that Seema had eloped with a boy from Jamkhi. The news came as the last nail, and the villagers could take nothing more. The entire Sarang village was up in arms. The villagers looked at this as a 'prestige' and 'honor' issue. Nobody was talking about peace . Samar's father was furious, and something serious was about to happen. The panchayat proposed to send a team to Jamkhi to ask the boy's father to reply and apologize. A few people left for Jamkhi to get the boy's family, and as they started heading towards the chauraha, more and more people joined the group.

Villagers in Jamkhi, on the other hand, were on the edge. They had sensed that something would go terribly wrong. They knew it was a gospel mistake, and the leaders of Sarang would never forgive. And then they got news that a big group of people from Sarang was heading to Jamkhi. In two minds whether to discuss or fight, people of Jamkhi decided to defend and fight for the boy's family. As the two groups came closer, seniors from Jamkhi tried to talk peace in an apologetic tone but soon sensed the anger in the crowd on the other side. Heated arguments followed, and eventually, the matter came to hand blows. The crowd became uncontrollable. Soon, everyone had to take a side, and your side was decided largely by one's religion and village of residence. In short, Jamkhi and Sarang were at a full-blown war with each other. Nobody was spared – the young and old, all were a part of the fight – some attacking and others defending. Soon, this fight spread across the Jamkhi village, and the unruly mob started torching houses. A couple of hours were full of mayhem.

Samar and Javed suddenly found themselves on opposite sides. Samar was extremely agitated, and for him, it was a matter of self-respect and pride. Javed, on the other hand, was dragged into this fight. The boy who eloped with Seema was from Javed's neighborhood, so as per the village norms, it was his duty to protect his family. Villagers were injured, and houses burnt. Nothing was spared, let alone friendship. Samar saw Javed trying to pacify him, but the situation wasn't easy for anyone to manage. After a couple of hours, the police arrived from the district headquarters and dispersed the crowd. Barricades were erected, and the movement of people from one village to the other was stopped. Samar's house was in complete mourning. His father took this as a personal insult, and the family was completely shaken.

For the next two days, there was an uneasy calm. Administration was on high alert, and senior civil servants visited the villages and met the villagers requesting peace. In a couple of days, things slowly started returning to normal. People again started working in farms, children started going to school, and life seemed to be coming back on track. For a few days, it was a bit tense, but tempers started cooling down. Samar had not met Javed for a while, so he was inquiring about him at their usual tea stall at the chauraha. What he heard shocked him even more. During the disturbances a week back, Javed lost his younger brother who died of severe head injuries. The family had another blow when their house was burnt down by an unruly mob. In a couple of hours, Javed had lost everything. His father was trying to control the mob and was seriously injured and hospitalized. In the aftermath, Javed and his family left Jamkhi and moved to the city.

Samar immediately left his cup of tea and headed to Jamkhi. His friend's house was reduced to rubble. All the houses in the neighborhood were destroyed by the mob. People had lost everything that they ever had. One incident had changed the life of so many. Samar came back home and was completely shattered. To begin with, the incident was a severe blow to him personally as he loved his sister. And the aftershocks of the incident took his friend away from him forever.

Since then, Samar and Javed never met each other. Samar tried to find the whereabouts of his friend in every possible way, but nothing worked. Life soon started getting back to normal, or at least it seemed to be. Farmers got back to fields and students to their schools. Samar completed his college and started helping his father in their fields. Evenings were, however, very dull for him. Though he had a few other friends and often joined them at the chauraha, he always missed Javed.

Years passed, and times changed. Samar's father handed over the baton to him, and now he was the Mukhia of the villages. Like his father, Samar also helped the villagers in every possible way. Soon, villagers started respecting and following him. As time passed, villages prospered with development all around. Now the villages had good roads and water supply. The chauraha was well-lit, and people could now chat until late in the evening as streets had sufficient light. There was hustle and bustle all around. But at the depth of his heart, Samar felt that loneliness. Over the years, Samar had many successes in life. He got married and was blessed with two sons. He prospered financially and added to their existing farmland by buying whatever he could in the nearby villages. Days were very busy, but evenings felt lull. The cup of tea in the chauraha soon was replaced with a glass of whiskey on the terrace of his haveli.

Life took a similar turn for Javed. The family fled the village after the tragedy and moved to Gurgaon, which was at the cusp of development. Small factories had mushroomed around the villages nearby, and Javed immediately took up a small job. He worked relentlessly, and after a few years, he bought a small shop along the highway. His hard work and commitment ensured that he walked the same lane of prosperity as his friend. Soon, his business expanded, and over a period of time, he opened a small factory near Gurgaon. Like his best friend, he too felt empty in the evenings. And as destiny would have it, the two friends accidentally came face-to-face in a mall this morning. It took less than a fraction of a second for them to recognize each other and just hug each other.

"How is Seema? Did she return later?" asked Javed while filling the third drink for both of them. Samar was absolutely quiet. As if he didn't want to talk at all on this subject, he was staring at the wall with a blank mind. Javed chose to brush the subject aside. He knew this was a sensitive topic and back then, it was a prestige issue in society more than anything else. The two friends finished their glasses and chose to stop for the day. After three decades, they had spent evening hours together. A lot had changed: the location, the environment and the drink. But the warmth was still the same. Javed then asked his driver to drop Samar to his residence. The two friends parted with a tight hug, and they were sure they would meet soon.

The doorbell rang the next morning, and Javed was a bit surprised as they hardly had visitors at home. He was astonished to see Samar at the door – finely dressed in whites like a seasoned leader. Javed welcomed him to the breakfast table and offered him tea. “Seema is in Gurgaon,” Samar said while sipping the tea, and the two friends locked their eyes on each other. “Three years after the incident, Seema had called me,” Samar continued. “She was blessed with a daughter, and I couldn’t wait to see them.” Samar then traveled to her place to meet her family. Over three years, his anger had mellowed down a bit, and it melted completely when he saw his niece crawling to him. His brother-in-law also welcomed him to their small house. While Seema was not as financially secure as in the past, she was visibly very satisfied. Her face was glaring with happiness when she realized that her elder brother had forgiven her for crossing the line.

While Samar had decided to welcome his brother-in-law into their family, he was very skeptical about their acceptance in the village. It was, therefore, decided that Seema would never return to the village, and Samar would visit her occasionally. Seems the village had forgotten her completely, and Samar didn’t want to remind anyone either. Soon Seema shifted to Gurgaon, and Samar would visit the family at regular intervals. He also helped his brother-in-law financially, and Seema got the same quality of life as in the past.

Javed was so happy to hear that. This morning was a completely different atmosphere. Samar then said, “I want to make one more decision: I want to gift you a small piece of land and a house in Sarang.” “Would you be ok to visit the village?” he asked. Javed was in tears. He got up and hugged his friend tightly, as if he never wanted to let him go. He immediately agreed to visit Sarang with his family in a few weeks’ time. The two friends had lost three decades of friendship due to an incident, but now they were in no mood to lose any chance to make up.

D'Silva House

D'Silva House, a majestic bungalow along a beach in the small village called Mangaon. The bungalow had 7 spacious rooms across 2 floors and a big lawn in the front. The backyard had a well that was never short of water. There was a small outhouse, more like a servant's quarter. The main gate opened on a small village road running parallel to the seashore. All the rooms on the first floor had a balcony facing the sea, and one could spend hours watching the beautiful sunset while sipping a drink. The bungalow was surrounded by many trees and provided shelter to hundreds of birds that made the mornings musical.

This huge property off late was very deserted. The only resident for this property now was Babu, an octogenarian who occupied the outhouse for more than 5 decades. He was a trusted servant of this home and has been around all the while: no holidays, no vacations and no other relatives. For decades, Babu spent all his time alongside Samuel D'Silva, popularly known as Sam in the village.

Sam was born and brought up in the village of Mangaon, a small sleepy village of about 100 houses. Largely an agricultural village, Mangaon was a calm and quiet village surrounded by vast lush green fields. Sam's father owned a huge farm outside the village, and the farm was filled with mango and jackfruit trees. He would spend most of his time during the day on the farm taking care of the trees and maintaining the farm. Before sunset, he would return home, now called D'Silva House, and spend time with his family. It was a small family of 5, and the three children would make it very lively. Sam was the eldest of the siblings, followed by Rohan (known as Ron), and Silvia was the youngest. It was a typical village home surrounded by a bamboo compound with lots of chickens roaming around.

Sam belonged to a religious, practicing Christian family, and every Sunday morning, they visited the church in the neighboring village. While returning, they would pick up weekly groceries and vegetables for themselves and as well as some neighbors. The D'Silva's were the only family in that area who had a car, and they were more than happy to help anyone during emergencies or any festivities. The family was, therefore, known and loved by one and all in the nearby area.

This fairy tale childhood suddenly hit a bump one day when Sam's parents were hit by a speeding vehicle one Sunday. Friends and villagers from the entire area gathered and prayed for them, but unfortunately, both of them died. Sam had just cleared his Matriculation exams then and was dreaming of joining a college in the taluka nearby. But now, he was left with another problem to solve – Ron and Silvia were too small and couldn't be left alone. Their farm and the business also required supervision. Sam, therefore, decided to pause his education plans and step into his father's shoes. As one of the village elders said, 'Sam grew from an adolescent to a matured young man overnight'. He was now the main support for his family and the farm.

Soon, Sam got used to a routine very similar to his father's. He would spend most of his day on the farm caring for the trees and fruits. Though tired by the evening, he would not hesitate to play with Silvia and Ron at home. Sam's father was loved by the entire village, and the villagers never left this family alone. People would visit them regularly and inquire about their well-being. Some would bring food and savories whenever they visited. The Father from the Church also visited the family regularly and spent some time with the kids. He felt very bad for Sam as he had to leave his education halfway but was also proud of his sacrifices for his siblings.

As years passed, Sam started becoming an expert in the agricultural business himself. Apart from mere jackfruits and mangoes, the farm now produced vegetables which added to the regular income. Sam developed some good contacts in the nearby taluka where he could manage a better price for the agricultural produce. Days passed by, but the routine was almost the same - get up early in the morning - prepare food for Ron and Silvia - drop them to their school - head to the farm - return back around sunset and spend some good time in the courtyard with his siblings.

As Sam entered his twenties, the Father of the Church convinced him to marry a beautiful girl from the neighboring village. The Father knew the family personally and was sure that the girl, Maria, would further strengthen the family. Maria was a great partner to Sam, and she helped him in every possible way. She managed the household tasks while Sam was busy on the farms, and that gave him time to explore opportunities in business. Ron and Silvia were growing up as well. Ron moved to the nearby taluka to complete his graduation and would visit the family every Friday for a weekend. Silvia chose to pause her education to help Sam and Maria in whichever way she could. Sam and Maria were blessed with two kids. A few years later, Silvia also got married within the village and stayed nearby. The D'Silva house was again bustling and lively.

While on his regular visits to the market, Sam met a young, energetic, and honest worker, Babu. Sam was impressed with his commitment to his work and his master. One day Sam asked Babu if he was open to working with him on his farms, and Babu agreed the very next minute. Soon, Babu became more like a part of the family. He would take care of the farms when Sam was out on some marketing trips. He was so honest and trustworthy that Sam could now spend a couple of days in the neighboring towns trying to build business relationships for his products. This whole support system helped Sam grow the business many folds and also make him financially stable.

Sam now wanted to build a bigger house – one that could give enough space for the increasing family and also leave enough space for fresh air and fun. Soon, Sam built a 'pucca makan' and named it 'Dsilva House'. As a gratitude to Babu for his commitment, he built a small outhouse behind the bungalow and requested Babu to stay with them. Babu was more than happy to be a part of the family. In one of his conversations with Sam, Babu asked Sam if it was worth spending so much building such a big house, Sam smiled and replied, "D'Silva house will keep the family together... always."

Just when everything seemed to be going well for the D'Silvas, a tragedy struck the family as Silvia's health started deteriorating. Despite all the efforts and prayers, the family lost Silvia after a brief illness. Nothing could describe the impact on Sam – he was so close to his siblings and couldn't accept such a big loss. Maria, however, stood by the family all the while. On one side, she supported Sam in this emotional tragedy and helped him come out of this. On the other side, she also took the responsibility of Rohit, Silvia's son who was just about a couple of years old and surely wanted someone to hold his hand as he grew. Maria was now his foster mother, and D'silva house again had three children playing in its courtyard.

As time passed, Sam accepted the reality and started getting back to the routine. He again started going back to his farms and soon got into his regular routine. Babu was a great help all the while. As a trustworthy lieutenant, he ensured that there was no lack of oversight even for a minute. Things started getting back to normal. Sam started concentrating on his work as usual, and the family got back to life. Ron completed his specialization and decided to take a corporate job in a city a few hundred kilometers away. He relocated to the city, but that was too far to visit every weekend. So his trips to Mangaon reduced to a monthly and later quarterly visit. His bond and affection for Sam, however, only grew stronger over the years. He loved his brother more than anything else. Unfortunately, he wasn't very keen on helping Sam in their farms, and a corporate job was more his calling. Sam knew this right from the initial childhood days, so he always motivated Ron to pursue his passion. Ron settled in the city, but D'silva House was always core to his heart.

Things settled down in the next couple of decades. Sam was busy with his work and was now known in his field. He would advise young guys who were keen to explore 'organic farming' as an entrepreneurial opportunity. Babu was standing next to Sam in all his endeavors. Maria was a fantastic partner to Sam, especially on the domestic front. The children grew up, and after schooling, they chose their paths. Amongst the three, Rohit, Silvia's son, was the closest to Maria and Sam. The bond among the three only grew over the years. Like his elder cousins, Rohit also completed his studies in the nearby taluka, but he never wanted to leave Mangaon. He joined his uncle Sam and started learning the tricks of farming.

As time passed, Sam started taking a backseat. Rohit now was the front face for the farms and the business, and he was groomed well by Sam and Babu. Over the years, Ron had a successful corporate run, and he soon retired from a very senior position. He had built a smaller version of 'D'silva House' in the city. Sam's children had also settled down well in their work in different cities. The family, in a way, was slightly disintegrated. D'silva House would now come to life only during festivities, primarily around Easter and Christmas. It was during these occasions that the entire family again gathered in Mangaon and spent some quality time together. The work had moved them to different locations, but their heart was always in the D'silva house and its patriarch, Sam.

One day, Sam got a massive heart attack and before anyone could act, he breathed his last. The family was in shatters. Like headless chickens, they were just too clueless on what's next. Everyone rushed home to join the last journey of the man who was the backbone of the D'Silvas and the D'Silva House. They had lost Maria a couple of years before but nobody could come to terms with losing Sam. After the funeral, they spent a couple of days at home, but nobody could stay there for long. Too many memories and whispers- they could imagine their childhood and how Sam and later Maria ran after them in the courtyard, how they spent hours in the garden and the farm. Everything was fresh in their minds, and it was difficult to come to terms with reality. Soon everyone started leaving back to their base. Ron and the children left for their respective homes in the cities. Rohit also decided to shift to his other house, the one built by Silvia and locked for many years. He couldn't imagine living in the D'Silva house without his uncle. Babu was the only one left in such a big property. He was growing old and decided to live in the outhouse as long as he was alive.

One day, in early December, Babu received a rare phone call – it was Ron. After inquiring about his health, Ron informed him that like every year, they all will be back in D'Silva House for Christmas. He, therefore, requested Babu to get someone to clean the house and get it ready for everyone. Babu was so thrilled to hear that. He got a couple of guys from the village and got the D'Silva House in shape. From the garden to rooms and the terrace, everything was cleaned as it was earlier. Some of the rooms were opened after a few months, so it was an effort in itself. However, the joy of seeing the house filled with people and laughter energized everyone, and D'Silva House was ready to host the usual Christmas holidays.

The family had a great week. Ron was the only sibling of the elder generation, and he was growing old as well. He had seen the D'Silva

House grow from a small hut to a sprawling bungalow. However, he was worried that Babu was too old to take care of the bungalow. There were occasional thoughts of selling the property, but given the emotional attachment, this thought never lasted for more than a minute. Ron was, therefore, very worried.

Soon, the holidays got over, and nobody remembered how the week passed away so soon. Everyone was planning to leave that afternoon post-lunch, and Babu was worried that he would now see a lively house only during Easter or probably next Christmas. Ron could easily notice a depressed Babu since morning.

At the lunch table, while everyone was busy planning for their travel and days to come, Ron had a thought, and he wanted to discuss that with the family over lunch. “The D’Silva House runs in my blood, and I am so happy to be here, even if it’s for a few days. I can’t forget even a minute that I have spent here. I just want to see this house remain intact as it always was,” Ron said. Two other people who were as emotional as Ron were Babu and Rohit. After a short pause, Ron continued, “to continue seeing this house as lively as it was and also in good maintained condition, I am proposing that we convert this house into a homestay. We will let out the rooms on the upper floor to a few families who want to spend a few days in the village across the seashore. Of course, that would mean some income, but more importantly, it will ensure that the house is lively round the year and also maintained. And who else can oversee and supervise this better than Babu? I am, therefore, suggesting that we open the doors of D'Silva House to the world and let people enjoy its warmth. What do you think, children?" Both Babu and Rohit were excited about the idea. Others agreed to the suggestion. As the family finished the lunch, they also decided on another important rule – Ron said, "we all will continue to visit D'Silva House every Easter and Christmas and ensure that the age-old tradition continues forever." Everyone agreed. Babu remembered Sam saying a few decades back, 'D'Silva House will keep the family together.'

Justice

IT WAS A PACKED courtroom in the High Court of the state capital. Many people were trying to get into the room, and the police were trying hard to keep them out of the court and prevent any chaos. A police van brought the 'accused' Mohan amidst tight security and escorted him to the court. In a few minutes, the judge arrived, and the proceedings started. The judge and Mohan looked at each other – they both could recognize each other, though they had come face-to-face after a very long time. The proceedings began, and the judge asked Mohan if he had a lawyer to represent him. Mohan nodded in the negative. Suddenly, there was a voice from behind, 'I am representing him' and everyone looked behind. A young girl in her late twenties was seen hurrying to the front. She identified herself as Supriya and was representing him in this case. Mohan was a bit surprised as he couldn't recognize her, and he knew he hadn't hired one, but the judge moved on. It was a case of murder, and Mohan was the prime accused, so he was remanded to custody and denied bail. The date was provided for the next hearing, and the case was adjourned until then.

Mohan was immediately taken by the police to the van standing by. Hundreds of villagers had gathered to show their solidarity with Mohan, and some even tried to block the way, but the police maneuvered their way and took him to jail. For some reason, Mohan was confused because he didn't hire any lawyer. On the contrary, he had confessed to the murder and even signed his declaration without any hesitation. Who was this lawyer, and why was she representing him? He, however, realized that it was going to be a long-drawn court battle that may go on for years.

The next day, Supriya visited him in jail and took some signatures on documents. After completing the documentation, he just looked at Supriya and asked her who she was and why she was fighting his case. He didn't have anything to pay her. She smiled and said, "Kaka, didn't you recognize me? I am Supriya Vaze. Savita's school friend Mohan was completely surprised. He was happy but also astonished to see her. She soon left, promising to come back in a few days to discuss the case and her plan.

Supriya was Savita's best friend. Both were schoolmates from the same village, and for years, they spent most of their days together. But he had seen Supriya after more than a decade, and a lot had changed. Mohan returned to his cell and took a trip down memory lane. He could clearly see those pictures. Until a few years back, he had such a wonderful life, and suddenly one incident changed it all for many in that village.

Mohan was a small farmer in the village of Sonpur. It was a small village with fewer than a thousand villagers, so almost everyone knew each other. Mohan had a small piece of land outside the village. Land in the village was fertile, and with adequate water in the river, farming wasn't very difficult. Sonpur was a closely-knit village with very few disputes or quarrels. The villagers lived like one big family.

Mohan was blessed with a beautiful daughter, Savita. She was studying in the school in the neighboring village along with other kids in the village. Her father was her world. Every morning, she would go to school along with her friend Supriya. She would come home straight from school and, after completing her studies, helped her grandmother in her daily chores. Before evening, the grandmother-granddaughter duo would complete all the work at home and wait for her father. After a laborious day at the farm, Mohan would come home before sunset, and the trio would have a cup of tea on their veranda and chat for an hour. Mohan would then visit the village center to meet other friends in the village before having his dinner. Mohan had lost his wife a few years back in an accident, and since then, he played the roles of both father and mother for Supriya. His entire effort was focused on the right upbringing of Supriya, and his mother was helping him in every possible way.

All in all, it was a wonderful phase of life for Mohan. A teenage daughter who loved him with no boundaries, a mother who managed the house perfectly, and a farm that produced enough for the family to lead a comfortable life. Mohan's neighbor Ramji was his good friend. Their houses shared a boundary wall, and his daughter Supriya was Savita's best friend.

They were all a single family, especially during festivals and religious events.

Time was passing by fast, and nobody was complaining. However, everything turned completely upside down in just a moment. Everything fell like a house of cards, and nothing was left. On a fateful afternoon, Supriya came home running. She was badly hurt and bleeding profusely. She was so terrified that it took some time for her to settle down and speak. Everyone had realized that something bad had happened, but nobody knew what. Villagers reached out to Mohan and Ramji, who left everything at hand and rushed home. While Supriya was yet to come to her senses and narrate her nightmare, villagers realized that Savita was missing. The entire village then set out in search. They looked at all possible locations – on the way to her school, the temple, fields, and the village center. She was nowhere to be found. Mohan didn't want to accept anything untoward for his daughter, and as the situation started being grim, he collapsed and fell unconscious. The doctor from the neighboring village visited, and after a while, Mohan seemed fine.

By this time, Supriya had calmed down. She saw almost the whole village around her, and that also gave her some sense of security and comfort. Everyone was waiting to understand what exactly happened in the afternoon and where Savita was. Mohan walked up to her. His eyes were filled with tears. He held her hand and asked, "Beta, do you know where Savita is?". Supriya couldn't control herself and burst into tears. The village elders stepped in and assured her that she was safe, and she should not worry about anything. They asked her if she knew anything that could help them find Savita.

Supriya then narrated the whole episode. Like any other day, the two friends were heading back home after school. They were chit chatting and enjoying their walk on a bright sunny day. Suddenly, a van stopped next to them on the road, and a couple of boys in the van started teasing them. The two girls were terrified and started hurrying their way home. The van overtook them and stopped with a sudden break. Two guys stepped out and started pulling the girls into the van. The girls struggled and pushed back; however, the guys were successful in overpowering Savita. They pulled her into the van and started following Supriya, who was now running for her life. Supriya soon ran into the neighboring fields and was followed by a couple of guys. She fell down a few times and hurt herself but continued to run with all her might. As she got closer to the village and started shouting, the guys gave up the chase and rushed back into the van. The van then picked up speed and went in the other direction.

Supriya saw the van heading out of the village. For a moment, she was relieved as she could save herself. However, the very next moment she realized that Savita was missing. In fact, she was hauled into the car and was helpless. Supriya was shouting for help at the top of her voice, but there was nobody around. She then started running home. She was horribly broken as she couldn't save her best friend. The Sarpanch, who was sitting next to her and listening to the story, asked her in a soft voice if she had seen any of those guys and if she knew anyone. After a few seconds, she said she had seen Jeetu in the van sitting next to the driver.

Everyone started looking at each other. "Jeetu... God save Savita," they said. Jeetu was the only son of Sangam Singh, a rich landlord of the neighboring village. He was a rich, spoiled kid who was known in the area for all the bad habits. Sangam Singh himself was famous in the area for all the wrong reasons like threatening villagers, giving loans against land and eventually grabbing the land, exploiting laborers, etc. The local police were fed up with complaints against Jeetu about molesting and teasing girls and women in the villages, but eventually, they always had to let him go as Sangam Singh was well connected in political circles.

The sarpanch immediately got up and asked Mohan and a few elders to accompany him to the police station. They formally lodged a police complaint. The police immediately got in action and started looking out for Jeetu. Everyone feared the worst, but nobody wanted to believe their fears. Soon, it was dark, and this was supposed to be the longest night for Mohan and Ramji. Supriya couldn't sleep the whole night and was terrified. Ramji feared something else – he knew Supriya was the sole witness of the event, which meant that the police would talk to her a few times about the incident. He also knew that eventually, she would be expected to be a witness in the case if it reached the court. He knew the might of Sangam Singh and his goons. All in all, he knew life was not safe for him and his family in the village now. Mohan, on the other hand, couldn't sleep the whole night and was restless. Soon after sunrise, he decided to personally search for Savita again. As he stepped out, he was surprised to see a lock on Ramji's door. Ramji had fled the village along with his family. Nobody knew where he was, and nobody saw them leave. Some even feared that Sangam Singh's goons would have kidnapped him, but Mohan was sure that wasn't the case, as he was awake the whole night and didn't hear any noise.

Soon, Mohan and a few others in the village started their search for Savita, and this time they also extended their search to the nearby forest area. The villagers left no stone unturned and searched in every nook and corner. And suddenly someone shouted from behind the woods. Savita's body was lying in a pool of blood. She was dead. The whole village gathered in the next few minutes and so came the police. The body was immediately taken by the police for further investigation. The fears of villagers came true. They lost their beloved daughter. Everyone knew who the culprit was, and everyone knew that he would be let free in a few days.

The police started the investigation, and soon the post-mortem report came. She was strangled to death, and the body was dumped in the forest late at night. The report also confirmed multiple sexual assaults on her. Everyone knew it was Jeetu and a few of his accomplices. Soon after the formalities, the body was handed over to Mohan for the last rites, the entire village gathered to bid a farewell. Ramji and his family were missing. While a few were anguished by his running away, many could appreciate the decision because they knew the threat to him and his daughter.

Jeetu had initially absconded but later surrendered to the local police. Soon, the hearing for the case started in the district court. Not many were surprised as one of the famous criminal lawyers from the city was representing Jeetu. His body language, command of the subject, and ability to argue on finer points were well known in legal circles. The public prosecutor was also a very seasoned and knowledgeable person but was often outpaced by Jeetu's advocate. The arguments went on for months with charges and counter-charges. As one of the leading legal luminaries once said, "In any case, the prosecution and the defense always know what the truth is, it's the judge who is on the trail." In this particular case, the judge was a very intelligent and sharp legal expert. From the very first argument, he knew who the culprit was, but he was waiting for the right arguments and representations. Unfortunately, the key witness, in this case, Supriya, was not available for any testimony. Despite efforts, the police could never trace Ramji and his family.

During all these hearings and court proceedings, the judge could see humble Mohan sitting in the first row in anticipation of justice for his beloved daughter. The judge could see clearly in his eyes. He could also see the anguish on the face of the villagers and the support they lent to Mohan all the while. What nobody noticed was a frail man with a long beard and a covered head present in all the sittings – it was Ramji. Out of fear, he had moved overnight to the neighboring district. He took up a small job in a local factory there. However, like Mohan, he never missed a single court sitting. Unfortunately, he could never gather the courage to look into Mohan's eyes. He knew Supriya's testimony was the key to this case, but he also feared that she would meet the same fate if they came out in the open.

But Ramji was a strong man. While he did what he did for his family, he ensured that Supriya was not only protected but also got into a local school. Every time after visiting the court, he would brief his family on what happened and how a strong lawyer was swaying this case against the truth. Supriya could feel his helplessness and agony. They knew they were being selfish. But at the same time, they were determined to set things right sometime in the future.

Everyone knew who the culprit was and what he had done. Unfortunately, the arguments of the defense lawyer always outperformed the prosecution, and the judge was forced to follow the rule books. Eventually, after years of arguments and hearings, the court finally had to let Jeetu go for the lack of evidence and witness. Heavens fell on Mohan, and he was completely broken. The entire village was upset as they felt that they had been deprived of justice. On the other hand, Jeetu was a free man. However, sensing the tempers in the village, Sangam

Singh sent Jeetu to his uncle's place abroad. He wanted to shield his son and also ensure that he completed his education with no roadblocks.

Years passed by, Mohan had started working in his field again. Unfortunately, during these years, he had lost his mother. He was now lonely – no family, no neighbors. The village had reconciled with reality and moved on. The incident faded in their memories, but they weren't ready to forgive Sangam Singh. Mohan continued to sulk in solitude. He wanted justice for his daughter. He also knew that it was difficult to fight legal battles given the might of the culprits. He simply didn't know what to do.

And then one fine day, there was news in the village that Jeetu was visiting the village for a few days. In fact, Sangam Singh had planned his wedding in the next few days. Mohan was restless. He couldn't believe that Jeetu was leading such a great life even after committing such a heinous crime. He simply couldn't come to terms with reality and was thinking continuously about revenge. Soon, he hatched a plan, and nobody could ever imagine how a simple farmer could think beyond his usual routine.

The village only had a couple of grocery shops, and Mohan knew the grocer who supplied stuff to Sangam Singh's bungalow. Over the next few days, Mohan visited the shop more often, and during casual conversations, he tried to gather as much information as possible. He now knew the date when Jeetu was expected to land at the nearby airport. He also knew that the international flight landed late at night, so by the time Jeetu would reach the village, it would be pitch dark. As in the last few years, he was silent and in himself without talking to anyone about anything.

And then came the fateful morning. The village woke up well before dawn, and there was complete chaos. Jeetu had been murdered! The entire village was surprised. Nobody knew anything. Everyone was aware that he had done all the wrong things in life, and many in the village hated him, but who had the courage to kill Jeetu and how! Police swung into action, and they knew it would be sensitive. The investigation started right away, and half the village was a suspect because most of them had a reason to hate him. However, the police knew that this would require more than a motive. An investigation revealed that the killer had some plans for a while.

Recreation of the crime revealed that Jeetu might have headed to his home from the airport past midnight. His driver picked him up in their car. The trap was laid a mile outside the village. It was an isolated stretch of road with absolutely no lights for almost a mile and small shrubs on either side of the road. Someone had kept the trunk of a tree across the road just around the turn. The placement around the turn was selected such that one could see the block only about 10 meters, which gave a little chance for the driver to stop or reverse the car. Eventually, the car crashed in the woods injuring the driver and Jeetu, who invariably sat next to the driver. However, not taking any chance, the killer also stabbed his throat with a sharp knife to ensure that he would die immediately. As the car had crashed and the driver lost control, there was very little resistance. Since Jeetu didn't reach home until the early hours, his family set out to search for him, and that's when the incident came to light.

The police largely knew 'how,' so the question was 'who' and 'why.' The entire village was searched, and the police shortlisted a set of villagers who were worst hit by Jeetu's behavior in the past. One such person was Mohan, whose house was searched thoroughly, but the police could hardly find anything. Similarly, searches in other premises also didn't yield anything. However, under pressure, the police arrested a few suspects and tried to pressurize them to get to the truth. Unfortunately, nobody knew anything and nobody confessed. Mohan's body language was, however, different; while he didn't confess anything, he was not repenting the incident, and that, in a way, was acting against him. The police, therefore, considered him as a prime suspect and arrested him.

The case came for hearing in the High Court. Mohan didn't have any money to hire a good lawyer and looked as if he would again be short-changed by a quick-witted lawyer. However, destiny had a different plan this time. The case was assigned to a judge who had heard of these names in the past and could immediately recollect some of the faces. He was the same judge who presided over Savita's murder case a few years back. That whole episode was crystal clear in front of his eyes. This time he wanted to make sure that not being able to afford a good lawyer didn't become a reason for not getting justice. Over the weekend, he invited his college friend for a cup of tea and narrated the whole episode of Savita's murder. He wanted to make sure that Mohan got some good help and advice this time. The judge's friend was a reputed but expensive lawyer. Mohan was a poor farmer and the lawyer wanted to make sure that people don't suspect Mohan in any way. He wanted to help Mohan but without being noticed, as people would suspect, and if he himself defended Mohan, things may not look right. He, therefore, asked for some time and agreed to work out a plan. He asked his associates to dig more information about the old case and characters involved. In a couple of days, he got to know that Supriya, who was a key witness in the earlier case, had just completed her law studies. He contacted her and worked out a plan. The plan was simple – officially, Supriya would be his lawyer and defend Mohan in the court. At the backend, she had a few seasoned lawyers and a strong law firm to help her with legal arguments and procedures. In short, the judge, through his old friend, ensured that Mohan didn't go without a fair representation this time.

The legal arguments started in the second sitting itself. Supriya, with her passion and support, secured bail for Mohan. It would be a long-drawn battle going for years, but at least Mohan had the peace to be at home and at work most of the time. He was back in the village, and he got a hero's welcome. Many in the village thought that he was framed by Sangam Singh and was actually innocent. Few in the village suspected that Mohan had killed Jeetu to avenge Supriya's death. However, nobody was complaining. They all knew that Mohan was denied justice earlier, and it was only fair this time. A few more things changed – Ramji returned to the village with Supriya. A few friends in the village decided to support Mohan, who was feeling lonely these days. The friends would now take turns and send food for Mohan every day. Justice was finally done.

The Return Flight

IT WAS ONE OF the happiest days in his life. Today, Ravi was being felicitated by the Industry Association for his remarkable success. In the last few weeks, his rags-to-riches story featured in almost every leading newspaper and magazine. The news channels tried hard to get an hour of his time and feature his advice to the aspiring youth. In a very subtle way, Ravi took the place of a 'Role Model' for many aspiring entrepreneurs. He has successfully led his start-up to a glorious listing of shares on the stock market. Of course, he was now a millionaire, but he carried many people with him on this journey and ensured they got their share of success. Ravi knew that he would need to address the attendees of the ceremony and was preparing some talking points. And then he suddenly remembered Mahesh and was determined to mention him in his path to glory.

The banquet hall was filled with dignitaries. The who's who of the industry was seated in the front rows. He climbed the stage to a standing ovation. What a proud moment for someone who heads one of the leading 'Fintech' in the town. Some very reputed banks and corporates were now his customers, and he was well respected in his circles. His success was remarkable, and the industry body, as a token of appreciation, felicitated him for his contribution to the industry. He was then requested to address the audience and share his 'Path to Success'. The entire crowd in the banquet hall, and a lot more on a live broadcast, were eager to hear him.

Ravi planned to speak his mind today, so he walked up to the podium without any paper or notes. While he was scheduled to address the dignitaries in the banquet hall, he knew his real audience were those hundreds of thousands of young aspiring entrepreneurs who were watching a live broadcast of the ceremony. Ravi started as a usual speech thanking the industry body and his colleagues for being with him during his journey. However, he soon changed gear and tone. He asked the forum, "how many of you know me as a successful millionaire leading a strong business model, raise your hands." No points for guessing, everyone in the banquet hall raised their hands. Then he asked, "how many of you know that this very month ten years back, I was admitted to an ICU because I had attempted suicide and was saved by a miracle, raise your hands."

There was a pin-drop silence in the hall. The audience was taken by surprise; people looked at each other. They all knew Ravi for his brilliance and business acumen. But nobody was aware that he had once attempted suicide. Everyone knew that the journey of a start-up to success is bumpy, but nobody knew that Ravi's journey had almost ended before it even began. They were all very keen to hear more from him, and Ravi promised to talk about all that.

Ravi took the audience almost 15 years behind the calendar. "Let me start with a respectful reference to Prof. Shastry, the man who anchored me not once but twice. Prof. Shastry was one of the lecturers in my engineering days. He has been a lighthouse for many students in the college. A simple man with basic rules in life. Absolutely no flamboyance, down to earth, simple in life, and easy to approach. His first advice to me was to join a good reputed company and spend 5-7 years learning the business techniques before venturing on my own. Like many in college, I followed Prof.

Shastry initially – he referred me to one of his ex-students who took me as his assistants. My corporate journey began almost the very next day I was out of college."

Ravi continued, "my initial journey was very short, though. I always wanted to do something on my own and felt claustrophobic in a typical corporate job. Within six months, therefore, I stepped out and started on my own. I had a brilliant idea and big plans to make that happen. I started working from the backyard of a small garage and assumed that like most big corporations, my company will also start from a garage and lead the technology world. Unfortunately, in three – four months, I realized that it's virtually impossible to survive without support, and support was very difficult to come by. So after almost a year, I gave up the idea and closed the set-up. By then I had exhausted almost all my savings but made some good contacts in the ecosystem. I soon closed down my venture and joined a friend who had a similar start-up venture and a slightly better idea. Soon that venture gathered steam, and I was very hopeful that we had cracked the nut. But the dreams hit turbulence when we realized that funding wasn't very easy. I had already exhausted my finances, but my father and a few relatives stepped in, and we stretched for a couple of years. Unfortunately, after a couple of years, my friend realized that the product wasn't working out and decided to wind up."

"I was at the most horrible crossroads in life. With almost nil bank balance, we sold our only house and shifted to a rented premise. I couldn't look into my parents' eyes – I had pushed their hard-earned savings down the drain. For the next six months, I tried hard to get a job and somehow manage a day. Unfortunately, when times are bad, you have very few friends. A job was difficult to get, and many friends had their own commitments and compulsions. After struggling for almost six months, I decided to give up and attempted suicide."

"But life had different plans," Ravi continued. "Though I attempted suicide, I woke up after a couple of days in an ICU in a hospital close by. Just when I had consumed pills, the neighbor knocked on the door to inquire about something, and since I wasn't responding, they raised an alarm, and I was moved to the hospital in time. The doctors revived me, and soon I was out of danger. I woke up to a fresh morning and saw the housekeeping maid cleaning the floor. She informed me that Dr. Mahesh took very good care of me in the last 3 days, and he visited regularly until I was out of danger. Dr. Mahesh was the RMO in the hospital. He was a young brilliant doctor who had passed out recently from the local medical college. He came from an extremely poor background. Having lost both his parents in his childhood, he had to work very hard to make ends meet. However, he had promised his dying parents that one day he would be a doctor and work for the society. He wanted to pursue Masters, but due to financial constraints, he chose to work as a resident doctor in the local hospital for a couple of years before embarking on his onward journey."

Ravi continued, "that day Dr. Mahesh came for a round in the morning, and he was visibly relieved seeing me out of danger. He didn't say anything, though it seemed that he wanted to. He got back to his desk at the end of the ICU and continued with his work. In the evening after his shift, he again walked up to me and inquired if I was feeling alright. I nodded, and he just smiled. The next day I was shifted out of the ICU to the general ward, and soon many of my friends and relatives visited me. One late evening, Dr. Mahesh again met me – I was supposed to be discharged the next day. I was still in a depressed mood, though I had reconciled to my situation."

After a few quiet moments, Dr. Mahesh asked me – "why would you give up?" I didn't have an answer – in fact, there was no answer. Dr. Mahesh then shared his story. He was orphaned at a very young age. As an only child, he was all alone when his parents died. The local trust offered him a bed in the dormitory along with lunch and dinner. He, however, had to work hard to pursue education and meet his other needs. As promised to his parents, he continued with his schooling, though he worked in a nearby restaurant post-school to get some money." Dr. Mahesh continued, "for almost six years, I worked 7 days a week, 365 days a year just for a bright future. Soon I could clear my medical entrance and got a scholarship for fees. Even then I continued to take some tuitions to get some money in hand. There were days when I slept half my stomach simply because I couldn't afford a full meal."

Ravi continued, "Dr. Mahesh had a long struggle in his life right from losing his parents in the school days till struggling for fees for his post-graduation. He, however, taught me two very important lessons in life – first - never give up, you don't know what life has in store for you and second – value what you have got because many others in the world haven't even got half of that.

The next day I was discharged. I went home and realized the mistake. My parents were so happy to have me back home. I didn't think about them even for a second before taking such a drastic step. I was ashamed of myself. The next morning, I decided to just leave the past and move on. I was thinking about how to rebuild what I had lost – I suddenly remembered Prof. Shastry. He had retired now, but I could manage his address from the college. In the week after, I visited him personally and spent a few hours there. I shared the whole story of the last few years, and he listened patiently." "Now what?" Prof. Shastry asked me. "I want to start again," I replied. He then said, "start as if nothing has happened. Forget the past and look forward. You have a lot of time to rebuild, so just decide and move." But 'how' was the question, and as usual, Prof. Shastry had an answer. He promised to talk to a few of his former students and get me a job. “don’t give up dreaming. If you can dream, you can achieve” Prof. Shastry concluded. I promised not to forget his words. Soon I got a job with a small company and decided to rebuild my life. I worked for a couple of years before rekindling my passion to build a world of my own.

Ravi went on, “ This time, I decided to plan everything scrupulously right from product to marketing approach to contingency in case it fails. While I knew there is always a chance to fail, this time there can’t be a ‘free fall’. Which means I had to plan for some back-up resources just in case there are headwinds. As I settled into the job, I also started thinking about some new ventures in parallel. I learnt that I can always continue to work while the idea and the model takes shape. I don’t need to leave a full-time job till such time there is enough traction and pace. This ensured that I had enough day work but also ensured a steady income while the venture was still taking shape.”

“In another 6 months, things started to change. The Fintech venture was taking shape and in the right direction. In parallel, I was learning new aspects in the job which were also helpful in the venture. I now knew how to carry your venture to the customers and get their buy-in. Soon, there were customers who were ready to experiment. As an easy follow-up, now there were investors who wanted to invest in the idea and help with finances. In another quarter, I decided that it was time to take this venture as a full-time activity and leave the job. I was reasonably secure on my finances and confident about my venture this time. I, therefore, chose a good time to quit. And more importantly, I quit with a smile and a handshake to keep all bridges open, should there be a need later."

Ravi continued, "for the next 3 years, it was a roller-coaster ride. It was a fine balance between getting funding and spending on the right things to make the product attractive. We saw a lot of ups and downs. Many customers rejected us at the last minute, but this time I was a bit more mature and accepting. I had learned that often, things are beyond your control and you must move on rather than taking it too personally. At the same time, I had also learned that every rejection is feedback to work on and fine-tune your offer. And finally, I knew, success is hard and slow to come by. With this approach, we found it very easy to evolve ourselves to the customer requirements and expectations. Eventually, we started making a space for ourselves, and the customer gave us a seat at the table. We added one customer at a time and made sure he was happy before we moved to another. We also ensure that we cross all bridges when it comes to satisfying our customers – a lesson I learned in my second innings when I worked for a couple of years."

Ravi concluded his speech by saying, "with our learnings, experience, and attitude, I knew this time I will succeed. It was just a matter of time, and since it was my second innings, I had all the patience. Slowly with every customer, our offering strengthened, and we became a known and respected player in the industry. My final certificate of success came a few days back when we listed our company successfully on the stock exchange, which is also a testimony of the trust and faith of hundreds of investors."

Ravi then took a pause and asked if the audience had any questions. One young man immediately raised a hand and sought his advice to the young aspiring entrepreneurs. Ravi was ready with the answer, "Firstly, as Prof. Shastry has said, never give up. You always have enough time on your side irrespective of what stage of life you are, so just don't bother. Keep doing what you want to do, and you will succeed. Secondly, most of us would go through some or other financial distress or struggle. That's a part of life and should be taken in true spirit. As a very successful entrepreneur has said, 'this too shall pass.' So just keep working harder, and you will be out of the woods. Also, value what you got in life and appreciate that a lot more people around you aren't as lucky as you are. So make the best of everything that you have in life and move on. Finally, life always gives another chance, but you will succeed only if you haven't failed at heart. Remember, 'you failing' is different from 'your venture failing,' and so long as you can get up and start running again, nobody can stop you from winning. In summary, you fail the day you accept defeat."

The Postman Rings Twice

"POSTMAN", AN EXTENDED FAMILY member in Indian villages, was one person who was always loved and wanted. Personified as someone who is humble, friendly, and who joins you in all your moments of happiness and sorrow, he was one visitor who was always welcome. People would wait for him to knock on your door and hand over a letter. A money order by a migrant worker to his family members was always accompanied by a small message, and the postman would spare every time to read this in detail and convey all the emotions. The recipients would wait for the message rather than the money, and the postman would never spare a chance to make them feel good.

Vansaigaon was one such village in the interiors of the country – a small village surrounded by a few hamlets supported by a small post office. The post office had two employees – the postman, Sakharam and the postmaster, Sanjayrao. They stayed in small houses next to the post office and by the nature of their job, they were known to almost everyone in the villages served by the post office. Sakharam was particularly loved by the villagers. They would confide in him if they were awaiting an important letter or money order, and he would assure them a prompt delivery as soon as it reached the post office. On occasions, he would change his regular delivery route to deliver any good news or an important letter to someone, and the whole village appreciated such gestures.

It was the month of September, and the rains in the region had subsided, and the fields were covered by a green blanket. Lush green fields and cool breeze just enthralled the atmosphere around. It was a good monsoon, so the villagers were visibly happy and optimistic about their harvest. As a routine, Sakharam would leave his post office with his bag full of letters and documents to deliver across all the villages. While on his return, he would pick up any letters dropped by the villagers in the post box. He would then sort them out in the post office and keep them ready for the pick-up van to collect and take to the district post office. On one such day, he collected all the letters from different post boxes across the villages and returned back to his post office. A small drizzle on his way ensured that he was drenched, so he quickly changed his clothes and helped himself with a cup of tea before sorting out the letters received today. He started stamping the letters as he sipped his tea. Suddenly, his eyes stuck on a small 'postcard' written in a slightly heretical handwriting. He just flipped it to see where it was supposed to go, and the address said 'To The God', nothing more than that.

Sakharam was already late for his sorting, and the pick-up van was expected any time. Not knowing what to do, he just kept this postcard aside and proceeded with the other letters. Soon, he completed his stamping and handed over the letters for onward delivery to the district sorting center. However, he retained that unconventional letter as it had something special, which made him curious. The letter was addressed to 'God' and seemed to be a mixed tone of anger and request. It was written by 'Uma'. It took a few minutes for Sakharam to understand who Uma was. Her sweet letter to 'God' started with a big complaint — God had already taken away her father, and now her mother was also sick. She didn't have anyone to play with as her friends weren't talking to her, and often she and her mother had to sleep hungry. She then requested God to help them else she would stop talking to him. Sakharam was restless after reading the letter. He could now visualize her face but didn't know much about the family. So he decided that the next day, after dropping his letters, he would try and find more details about Uma and her mother.

Uma was an eight-year-old girl from Varagaon, which was about two kilometers from Vansaigaon. Her father was a daily wage laborer who would travel to the nearby town every morning in search of work. Her mother was a farm laborer. They lived in a small house in the village. Uma studied in the village school in Vansaigaon and would walk to the school along with a few of her friends. After a day-long work at the farm, Uma's mother would return late afternoon every day, and then they would spend a lot of time together. Chit-chatting about anything and everything, Uma's mother would prepare some meals for the family. Her father would normally come back late in the evening after a hard day's work. On a good day, he would get enough work to get some small toy or dress for Uma. The family would sit together in the small veranda in the evening for dinner. A small happy family and Uma were living a fantastic childhood.

Tragedy struck the family a couple of years back when Uma's father died in a road accident, and the family lost its key support. The whole village then turned on to support Uma and her mother. The landlord assured her of her job and also increased her wages. The village Sarpanch assured them that the fees and other education expenses for Uma would be taken care of. Neighbors often shared sweets and savories made on occasions and ensured that they didn't feel left out. Life was returning to normal for Uma and her mother. That's when tragedy struck again – Uma's mother was sick for a few days, and her cough refused to die down. Finally, she visited a health care center in the neighboring town where she was diagnosed with tuberculosis.

The news spread like wildfire in Varagaon, and people started avoiding the mother-daughter duo. Her mother lost her job, and the source of income dried up. Neighbors soon stopped talking to them with a fear that they may get infected. No more sweets for Uma, and her friends were all gone. Her mother's health was deteriorating day by day. Sakharam also got to know that often Uma and her mother would just have a glass of boiled water for dinner unless someone kept a plate of food on their veranda. He was visibly disturbed. He couldn't sleep that night. TB was a dreaded disease in the village, though it was curable. However, the majority of villagers were illiterate and instead of avoiding the disease, they would avoid the patient.

The next morning, Sakharam woke up to a new promise. He wanted to make sure he put Uma and her mother's life back on track. So, he picked up a pen and wrote a 'reply from God' to Uma's letter. In that letter, 'God' assured Uma that her mother would recover soon so long as she took medicines properly. Sakharam then picked up all letters to be dropped and headed to the villages to complete his daily job. Post dropping letters, he visited the local healthcare center and met the doctor. The doctor knew Uma's mother's case as he had himself examined her. Appreciating Sakharam's good intentions, he packed medicines for the next one week and handed them over to him. Sakharam then went to the only local grocer in the village. He picked up some rice and lentils that would feed the mother-daughter duo for the next three-four days. He did not forget chocolate for Uma. He then headed to Uma's house and stopped his cycle a few meters away from the house to avoid any disturbance. He quietly went near the house and left the food and medicine packets on the veranda. He also kept two envelopes – a 'reply from God' and another blank if Uma wanted to write another letter. He then went back to his post office.

The next day, after dropping all his letters, Sakharam visited the village Sarpanch. The two knew each other so they had enough to talk about. Sakharam then raised the topic of Uma and told the whole story. Sarpanch was moved by Uma's plight. Moreover, he felt ashamed that a postman who came to the village a couple of years back felt so much for Uma and her mother whereas the village had ignored its own daughter. He immediately got up and got ready. Both of them walked to the temple square in the village center – a place known for a few seniors of the village to gather and chitchat. The villagers had a brief discussion with the Sarpanch and the postman, and it was agreed that every day, one of the houses in the village would provide a fresh meal to Uma and her mother. Some villagers were a bit worried about the disease, but the sarpanch assured them that they just had to keep the food in a basket on the veranda, and that wouldn't be any issue.

Uma and her mother now had a full meal. Every morning, they got a basket of fresh roti-sabji that would suffice for the mother-daughter for the day. The medicines started showing positive results, and she soon started feeling better. The postman often visited them but chose to avoid knocking on the door. He would just keep a packet of biscuits or sweets or chocolates for Uma and leave without making any noise. Days went by, and Uma's mother was recovering fast. One fine day, the postman picked up another postcard written by Uma to God. This time, however, her tone was very different. She was so happy and full of life. She thanked God for helping them and also bringing them close to the villagers again. Sakharam was visibly happy and satisfied. Uma didn't know who her actual 'God' was, but that didn't bother Sakharam at all. He was happy that he fulfilled his duty as a postman and ensured that the message reached the right people at the right time.

In today's age, especially in cities, the role of a postman is diminishing. Letters are now replaced by emails and messages on phones. Money is now transferred online, and the postman visits so occasionally that many of us don't recollect his face. Ironic, that the world is coming closer, but such a humble member of our family is slowly moving away.

Sarathi

THE HIMALAYAS HAVE BEEN an attraction for many generations. This vast mountain range stretches across more than 2500 kilometers, touching many states from Kashmir to the northeastern parts of India. Gigantic yet peaceful, these mountains are covered with thick forests and have pulled tourists from across the world. Small hamlets on these enormous mountains have been popular with many tourists who are in search of peace and tranquility. Manali is one such beautiful town located at the northern end of the Kullu Valley, approximately 6500 ft above sea level. Snow-capped mountains are just a few kilometers from Manali.

Ritesh was always fascinated by these beautiful, calm hill stations. He wanted to escape from the busy life in Delhi and spend some time in the hills. Being a banker in Delhi, he had a very tough and demanding schedule. Apart from long working hours, the daily commute to the office drained him physically as well as emotionally.

At times, even weekends were consumed by the spill-over of office work, adding to his frustration. Finally, one fine day, he decided to take a break and head to Manali with his wife Reema and daughter Reshma. The objective was simple – be with yourself amidst nature and serenity.

The family flew to Chandigarh, approximately 250 km from Delhi, and then took a cab to drive to Manali. Ritesh particularly wanted to avoid driving himself as he wanted to enjoy the route to Manali. It's a long drive from Chandigarh, so the family was a bit worried initially. They soon hopped onto the cab, and their driver, Kamaljit Singh, made them feel at ease. He was a local Chandigarh cab driver who regularly accompanied tourists to the mountains. "You can call me Kamal, and I will be with you for the next 5 days. I will ensure a safe and peaceful trip all along, so just be assured and relax," he said to Ritesh. The family immediately struck a chord with Kamal.

Their journey began, and within an hour from the airport, it was a very different scene. The busy city roads were now behind them, and they were driving through rural Punjab. After a couple of hours, they entered the beautiful state of Himachal Pradesh, and the climate and environment changed completely. One would start seeing mountains around, a lot of greenery, and fresh water along the streams. This was such a different India compared to a busy city like Delhi. Fresh air, open spaces, trees, and streams all along. Kamal would share some local inputs around the places and their peculiarities to keep the family interested.

After about a 3-hour drive, they stopped at a local 'dhaba' for a quick bite. Ritesh particularly wanted to avoid posh restaurants and taste local food along the roadside dhaba, and Kamal knew many such good places to eat. Delicious but sinful food soaked in homemade butter simply took them to a different level of satisfaction. Soon they resumed their journey again. As they started getting closer to Manali, the climate changed. Despite being a bright sunny afternoon, one could feel a cool breeze. On their left was a mountain edge, and on the right, they could see the deep valley. Occasionally, they could see streams of water flowing along. It took them almost 4 hours to cross the tough terrain, and finally, they reached Manali. It was evening time with fading lights, but one could see how different it was.

Peak summer, but the temperature was in higher single digits. The family immediately clung on to their warm clothing. They checked into a beautiful room; the balcony had a view of the valley, and one could spend hours on this balcony. They decided to relax for the rest of the day and leave for some local sightseeing the next day.

The next three days were supposed to be full of 'me time' and 'family time' for Ritesh. He had decided to keep himself off his emails and phone calls. The family woke up to a chilly but fresh morning. It was a complete contrast to the usual Delhi morning. Temperature in single digits, and one could see fresh snow on the mountain tops from the balcony. It was a very clear morning, and they could see the beautiful hills and forests with small villages and townships in pockets.

A cup of tea with such a pleasant sight was more than what one can expect. As planned, Kamal reached the hotel at around 10 am to pick them up for a day-long tour. Kamal had all the plans in place to ensure that they make the best of their short stay in Manali. Committed as he was, he wanted to ensure that the family enjoys every minute of their vacation. "Where are we heading, Kamal?" Ritesh asked with curiosity. "Two targets for the day," Kamal immediately responded – "we will experience snow at Rohtang Pass and go through the Atal Tunnel."

Ritesh was excited to hear that. He had heard that Atal Tunnel was recently inaugurated and was the world's longest tunnel connecting Manali and Leh. It would be a pleasure to see this engineering marvel. Of course, the bigger excitement was to enjoy snow – something that you seldom do in India. It was a good 3-hour journey, but Kamal ensured a smooth and comfortable ride. Like other tourists, they rented a few warm clothes and moved towards Rohtang. As they started climbing up, it got colder. Soon they could see snow on either side of the road. This is rare, and the family was mesmerized to see this. The roads were a bit wet, so Kamal was driving at a very slow pace and took no chances.

Soon, the family reached the spot and stepped out to walk on the snow. For the next hour, they were just on the snow. His daughter Reshma just couldn't believe her eyes. Before this, she had seen snow only in movies so today was her day to see how it feels. The family also ventured into stuff that they would otherwise never do – skiing and riding a Yak. Within a few minutes, they realized that skiing wasn't their cup of tea. After a few falls and dashes, they gave up. But it was an experience worth its time. Reshma now wanted to take a few pictures with a yak. The yak is an enormous beast, and it's natural to feel intimidated at first sight. But Reshma soon realized that it's a very calm and friendly animal. She took a short ride and was thrilled. This was slightly different from a typical horse ride she had done a few times before so this was an experience to remember. They spent a couple of hours and realized that Kamal had come searching for them. It was already around 3 pm, and he was very keen that they leave now as it would be dark before they get back to the hotel. They soon started their return journey. They were exhausted but very satisfied. They stopped for a short snack break and headed back to the hotel. Kamal was right; it soon started getting dark, and visibility was an issue. "It gets dark very soon on the hills, and since the curves are a bit tricky, I requested you to return," Kamal tried to justify his suggestion. By evening, they reached the hotel, tired and ready to die in bed. Kamal had met their expectations and ensured that it's a fun-filled day. After a quick dinner, Ritesh went to bed as early as 9.30 pm. While retiring in his bed, he was wondering when was the last time he slept so early in the day. Clearly, he had a tough few months and this was a welcome break. The family was now looking forward to the plans for the next day.

Ritesh woke up very early the next morning – absolutely fresh and excited. He grabbed a cup of tea and stood in his favorite place – the balcony – staring at the valley and enjoying the Manali chill. After a couple of hours, the family got ready for their day out and Kamal was waiting to welcome them. "What's the plan for today?" Ritesh couldn't wait to hear that. Kamal smiled and gave a few options which included a visit to Kullu valley, a museum, hot water springs near Kullu, and Bijlee Mahadev – a Mahadev temple located on top of the mountain. The family seemed to be inclined to visit the temple though Kamal had some views. The temple was located on top of the mountain, and the view from the place is simply amazing. However, it is situated at an altitude of ~8000 ft and the vehicle would take you only till the last 2 km. Which means, the family would need to trek almost 2 km along the mountains. While it was a safe walk, and the temple had many visitors throughout the day, it was exhaustive. It's all the more treacherous if you aren't used to walking at altitudes. Kamal was, therefore, insisting that they look for other options, but Ritesh and Reema had made up their mind. So, like an obedient driver, he took the cab on the route to Bijlee Mahadev, a drive of almost 90 minutes from Manali.

Like yesterday, this drive was extremely pleasing. After crossing the initial traffic of Kullu and the nearby villages, they started the steep climb on the mountain. On both sides of the road were apple orchards, and Kamal stopped at one such place to show the family a few tiny fruits. At a closer look, the tree had hundreds of small, tiny apples. It was the initial season, and by autumn, the tree would be full of sweet Himalayan apples. Ritesh took a few close photos of tiny apples, and then they started moving up. Like the other day, as they moved up, the environment started changing. It became cooler and slightly windy. Eventually, they reached the parking spot, and Kamal parked his car near a small shop. He then guided the family to the path to climb the remaining path. For the last time, he indicated that it would be a slightly difficult trek, so if they wanted to rethink, this was the time. Ritesh was very keen to continue, so they picked up some basics like water and a shawl and started their journey. It was about 11 am and a bright sunny day. 2 km by itself is an easy walk for many, but this was different as it was along steep terrain. After walking for almost half an hour, the family realized that it was going to be a tough day and the walk wouldn't be easy. On their way, they could see a few visitors in the other direction – they had climbed early in the day and were now heading back. On inquiry, they understood that it typically takes about one and a half hours to walk along the route. After some time, they took a small break and sat on some of the rocks aside. They gulped some water and decided to rest for a few mins. The wind was blowing, and the sound was threatening. The route was covered with forest on either side, so the noise of leaves and branches swaying to the wind was deafening. A local villager passed by and he advised them to pick up pace and move fast. He said, "Pahadon mein mausam badalte der nahi lagti jaldi chalo" (Climate on the hills change in a few moments.. better to move fast and reach the destination). Ritesh was now wondering if his decision was right. It was still a long way, and the winds were only becoming stronger. The family, however, started walking with an objective to reach the temple. They were told that there are a few dhaba near the temple that would be a good place to rest.

As they were walking hastily, they could see Kamal running along the route. In a few minutes, he joined the family on their trek. When Ritesh asked, Kamal explained to him that it would be impossible for the family to make it alone if it rains. Generally, it gets very slippery and dangerous after it rains, and Kamal knew that the family would need some help and guidance. He felt it was his duty to join them as this was their first time in Manali. Ritesh looked at Kamal and couldn't help appreciating his gesture. Soon the family started walking fast to reach the temple as fast as they could. Going up was now the only option because they had already crossed half the way. As they got closer to the dhaba, it started raining, and in a couple of minutes, it started raining heavily. They literally ran a few meters and rushed into a small dhaba, which was nothing more than a tent covered with plastic. The owner immediately got them some chairs to sit and prepared some hot tea. After a short break and a wonderful cup of tea, they decided to resume their journey as the temple was just about 200 meters. Kamal chose to stay back at the dhaba, and the path was now less risky so they were fine. It was still drizzling, and the path was now very slippery, but the family started walking towards the temple.

As they reached the temple, it was an experience by itself. The temple was located on top of one of the highest peaks in the area, and they could feel the clouds passing by. The trust had made adequate arrangements for the pilgrims, and the temple was very well maintained. However, due to the storm, there was a power shutdown. The temple was adequately lit with lamps, so they could get a glimpse of one of the most auspicious and sacred Shivlings. The priest was very humble and appreciative of all the pilgrims who visited the temple in such a climate. After sitting in the temple for a few minutes, Ritesh decided to step out and get back to the dhaba below. However, it was now a different situation outside. It was completely dark, and nobody would believe it was 2 pm in prime May. It was so cloudy that one couldn't see beyond 10 meters. The temperature was in the higher single digits, but the blowing wind on top of the mountain made it feel even lower. One of the employees of the temple realized the situation and opened the doors of one of the dormitories behind the temple. He requested all the visitors to move to the room and make themselves comfortable. There were adequate blankets in the room, so Ritesh, Reema, and Reshma quickly got inside blankets to feel the warmth. Ritesh was a bit worried now.It was already mid-afternoon, and the climate was such that he thought they might need to spend the night there. In another 10-15 mins, Kamal came searching for them. Seeing him, the family felt an inch comfortable. He informed them that the situation has improved a bit. It has stopped raining, so they could walk up to the dhaba below and wait there for a few mins. He expected that the clouds would move swiftly given the wind, and they could trek down soon. Ritesh decided to go by his wisdom, and the family soon reached the dhaba. Kamal had already asked the dhaba owner to keep some firewood and tea ready for them, so as soon as they were inside, they felt at ease.

After about 15 mins, they realized that it was a clear sky now with bright light-good enough to walk down. Kamal requested the family to move swiftly so that they could climb down before it's dark. They started walking along the steps. It was still cold, but with no rains, it was a bit bearable. Moreover, as they started walking through the forest, the impact of wind reduced, and they could walk comfortably. Raindrops had made it a bit difficult to walk along, though, and it was very slippery. But Kamal was along with them all ready to support and even hold the backpack for some time. Climbing down was surely easier and quicker than trekking up. Moreover, the fear of getting stuck halfway encouraged the family to continue going without any break to relax.

After about an hour and a quarter, the family completed the trek and reached the parking lot. They stepped into the car and phew, they were so relaxed. For a couple of hours, they were nervous about getting stuck amidst the forest, but now they were in the car, they were sure they would reach safely. Now that the anxiety was off, they got back to their senses, and the first thing they realized was the stress in the legs due to the climb. Muscles had already started paining, and that was an indication of the effort they had taken today. However, the scenic beauty outside made them forget the strain and enjoy the valley. The family was now visibly relaxed, but Kamal was still a bit worried. "We should be okay now, right Kamal?" Ritesh tried to sniff why he was worried. "Sir, it's a long drive down the mountain, I am worried if it rains, the wind may have uprooted any tree! However, the villagers here help when such instances happen, so we should be safe now. Don't worry," Kamal replied. Kamal continued to negotiate the sharp curves and steep terrain, and the family kept on enjoying the route. Reshma was a bit too tired, so she just slept in the back seat while Ritesh and Reema continued to enjoy the fascinating beauty around.

By around 6 pm, the family was back at the hotel. It had been a rather adventurous day for them, but looking back, it was worth all the effort. Apart from getting a glimpse of a sacred Shivling, they got an experience of how it feels getting stuck amidst forests during unexpected rains. Almost a 4 km trek was also a difficult task, but they had done it. All in all, it was a memorable day, and the family couldn't thank Kamal for all his efforts today. "Thanks, Kamal, for all your hard work today, without you, we wouldn't have made it safely," Ritesh acknowledged. Kamal responded humbly, "That's my job, sir, how can I leave you halfway!" Kamal added, "Tomorrow is planned as a day to relax for you all. You can spend the day along the Mall road or visit a monastery nearby. It's all walkable, and we can't take the car there. I will take the car to a local garage today just to get it cleaned and checked. Day after tomorrow, we will head back to Chandigarh. Hope that's fine." "Yes, we are good," Ritesh replied, and the family retired to their room. After a quick shower, they spent a couple of hours on the balcony recounting the day and how it went.

The next day was a day to relax and chill in Manali. The family roamed around Mall Road and visited the famous Hadimba temple, a couple of kilometers from the Mall. They picked up a few souvenirs on the way and treated themselves to some authentic Tibetan food. The evening was largely restricted to their balcony to spend time amongst themselves and chitchatting. They knew tomorrow was again a long day – the family was scheduled to drive to Chandigarh and then take a short flight to Delhi to close the vacation. Ritesh was so relaxed in the last three days that he wanted to stay on for another few. But he knew that all the good runs end someday and he will need to get back to the office soon.

The last day started a bit early as they wanted to start as early as 7 am to avoid any delays. Like always, Kamal was waiting for them outside, and he immediately helped them with luggage, etc. As the family started the return journey, Kamal warned them, "Sir there is a small bad news – there has been a landslide along a mountain on the way yesterday. The authorities worked till late evening, and the path was cleared for traffic, but the travel would be very slow given the silt and damage to the road. It would be a slightly bumpy ride." Ritesh was a bit worried, but then he knew Kamal would manage things well and get them safely to the airport.

It was indeed a slow drive along the ghat. One could see the remains of the mud and boulders along the other side of the road, so practically only half the road was operational for two-way traffic. But what a contrast – despite so much traffic and so many vehicles, it wasn't as noisy or stressful. All the drivers – buses, trucks, cabs, private vehicles – followed some kind of discipline and avoided any overtakes to land others in a problem. No horns, no abuse, no shouting, everyone trying to negotiate the difficult part of the road and also accommodating the others. Ritesh was wondering what happens to the same drivers when they reach cities!!

Anyways, the drive continued safely, though it took a couple of extra hours. Ritesh remembered Kamal saying at the start of their journey at the beginning of the week that it's always better to keep a couple of spare hours along the mountain ghats given the nature of the route. This advice came in handy during the end of their trip, and the family could reach the airport on time. Ritesh had already paid Kamal but couldn't help giving him more. Apart from tipping him for all his hard work, they had also picked up a souvenir for him from the Mall Road, and he was so happy to see that. It was Ritesh's way to thank Kamal for ensuring that their trip was uneventful and comfortable. Like they said in the past, *'To win the war, you need a capable 'Sarathi',*' in today's world, a *sarathi* like Kamal is worth his weight in gold.

Success Is What You Define

NOTICEABLE CHAOS OUTSIDE THE ICU of a reputed private hospital in the town—the district's most reputed jeweler, Santosh Singh, got a massive heart attack while at work and was rushed to the hospital. At least eight to ten of his employees accompanied him to the hospital along with Santosh Singh's elder son, Satish. His daughter Sunita, who was married to a reputed industrialist in the nearby town, was on her way to meet her father. Santosh Singh was in an unconscious state, struggling to breathe, and the doctors at the hospital hurriedly set him up in the corner section of the ICU.

Santosh Singh was a third-generation jeweler in the district town of Bharatnagar, a small but prosperous district in Rajasthan. His grandfather had set up a small jewelry business almost 75 years back, and his father carried the legacy successfully for years. Santosh Singh took over the business almost 25 years back when his father expired. Since then, he has spent every possible minute leading this business to a different scale. From a small shop in the city center, he now had a chain of 20 shops across three neighboring districts. Today, he employed more than 250 people across all his setups. And post-aligning with a couple of reputed online retailers, his business now was not restricted to any geography. A shrewd businessman, Santosh Singh was known for his acumen and foresight. However, he was more known for his philanthropy and social contributions. He funded the education of many poor people in society. His temple trust was known to be feeding many poor villagers across the district daily. For Santosh Singh, his 250 odd employees were a part of his extended family, and they were free to approach him in case of any problem.

Santosh Singh was proud of his success; for him, success was defined by two parameters—the amount of money you have and the number of people who bend to pay their respects to you when you walk. In both counts, he had no parallel in the district. Born in a small independent house in the city, Santosh Singh had built a huge castle for the family outside of Bharatnagar. The family had a luxurious life with four high-end sedans and a group of domestic helps to manage the chores. His elder son, Sunil, had graduated almost fifteen years back but joined his father in the family business even before that. People would say Sunil was a clone of Santosh Singh, especially in his business intuition. The youngest of his children, daughter Divya, was happily married. Her wedding was an extravaganza that many in the town would never forget. The younger son, Satish, was the only exception and regarded as a 'black sheep' of the family.

Satish differed from Santosh and Sunil. He was more into books and studies, showing no inclination towards business. The only occasions he visited the showrooms were during Diwali for the pooja. He completed his twelfth standard and expressed a desire to study in the nearby city. Santosh Singh was furious upon learning his choice, as he always thought both his sons would join the business and help take it to unimaginable heights. Adamant as he was, Satish didn't relent to any pressure and eventually moved away from Bharatnagar. With ever-increasing differences with his father, Satish kept drifting away from the family. The only bridge in the last five years was Sunil, who loved his younger brother and never allowed him to break away.

Santosh Singh was now admitted to the ICU and was being examined by the resident doctors in the hospital. The chief doctor grasped the gravity of the situation and recommended summoning the consulting cardiac surgeon in an emergency. Fortunately, the surgeon arrived within a few minutes, initiating a detailed examination. He then prescribed a few IV fluids, which were promptly administered. In a couple of hours, Santosh Singh began feeling comfortable. He regained consciousness within a few hours, bringing a big sigh of relief to the family.

The next morning became a family affair. Daughter Divya had reached the hospital and sat beside her father. Sunil had just arrived with fresh flowers and fruits. Santosh Singh appeared visibly healthy, engaging in conversation with the family members. The family recounted the previous day's nightmare. Santosh Singh then inquired, "Can I meet the doctor who saved me last night? He is my angel." The nurse mentioned that the doctor typically conducted rounds to meet patients around 10:00 am. The family was eager to express gratitude to the doctor for his efforts.

The doctor entered the ICU at 10:15 am, and as Santosh Singh saw him, his expression changed completely. The entire family was dumbfounded as the doctor approached Santosh Singh and examined the reports. After signing observations, the doctor provided instructions to the nurse and signed the sheet. As he was about to leave the room, Sunil held his hand and said, “Not today.” The doctor turned back to see Santosh Singh almost in tears. Someone known for strength and stubbornness at heart was on the verge of tears. “Satish...” he said, and the doctor touched his feet and broke down. Santosh Singh pulled him to his chest, and they wept. After a few minutes, they calmed down, and Satish left the ICU to meet a few other patients.

Santosh Singh saw Satish after almost a decade. He was upset that his son refused to join his business, leading to their drift apart. Satish had moved to the nearby city and pursued medicine. After completing his graduation, he moved to Mumbai for his Masters. A couple of years back, he returned from Mumbai and started practicing as a consulting cardiologist in the neighboring town. He was always keen to move back to his native place but wanted to avoid Bharatnagar for obvious reasons. His humility and commitment made him an instant success in this small town. Sunil was always in touch with his younger brother, much to the ignorance of Santosh Singh. Yesterday, when Santosh Singh suffered an attack, Sunil first reached out to Satish, who suggested bringing him to this hospital. Meanwhile, Satish left all his appointments, rushed to the hospital, and reached in no time. The brothers ensured that the 'golden hour' was not wasted, hence facilitating Santosh Singh's speedy recovery.

In the next few days, Santosh Singh recovered and was moved out of the ICU. During his stay, Satish regularly visited, reviewing all his reports and health parameters. They exchanged pleasantries, yet an uneasy calm and a glass barrier persisted. Meanwhile, Santosh Singh interacted with the hospital staff and discovered that Satish was a known and well-respected cardiologist in the region. His dedication and commitment to work were unparalleled. He had saved many people from almost certain death, ensuring their return to good health. Whether it was odd hours, weekends, or festivals, Satish never hesitated to reach any associated hospital if needed. He shared one thing in common with Santosh Singh—his commitment to society and the underprivileged. He was ever willing to forego his fee if the patient was from a poor family, even paying bills for patients facing financial challenges. Santosh Singh witnessed instances where patients or their relatives didn't hesitate to touch Satish's feet in gratitude and respect.

Throughout his life, Santosh Singh believed that Satish was unlike him. Money and a fancy, luxurious lifestyle didn't fascinate Satish. He confined himself to books and studies, always keeping a distance from the family business. Thus, Santosh Singh thought Satish was very different. But was he? Well, he was as successful as Santosh Singh, albeit in a different field. The underprivileged looked up to him for support, and like his father, he never let them down. Santosh Singh soon realized that Satish was equally successful, although his definition of success and respect differed from his father's. Sunil was eager for the father-son duo to talk and bury their differences. He envisioned his brother being part of their palatial house and a big, happy family. Santosh Singh, however, refused, now understanding that Satish was equally successful in his life, if not more. He also acknowledged that they both had different parameters to measure life and success. He didn't want to interfere or influence his younger son any longer. Soon, he was discharged and stepped out of the hospital, a proud father as both his sons were doing very well in their aspirations.

Diametrical

BOM-DEL - THE MUMBAI-DELHI air sector is supposed to be amongst the top five busiest routes globally. Nearly hundred flights between the two cities carry thousands of passengers each day. Some travel for business, others for short vacations, or to meet their families. Most of the flights run at full capacity with passengers in different moods. Some are nervous about their forthcoming meetings, a few excited to meet someone on arrival, few in a pensive mood while a few others are just waiting to get across the city. The return journey for many could be very different depending on how things transpired in the other city.

Shobha was traveling on one such flight from Mumbai. She was staring out of her window seat and desperately waiting for the plane to take off. She looked a bit disturbed and worried. Shobha was a working professional in Mumbai, associated with a leading advertising agency. She had crazy schedules and hardly had time for herself or her family. She was visibly tired as she had returned from a hectic trip just the last evening and had to rush to Delhi this morning. Almost motionless, she was keen to reach Delhi as soon as possible.

Shobha was in deep thought when suddenly someone tapped her. It was Simran, the girl seated next to her in the middle seat. They didn't know each other, but the outgoing and outspoken Simran hardly required any connection. Sitting next to someone during a 90-min journey was a good reason for her to talk to you.

"Hi, I am Simran," she said with her right hand waiting for acknowledgement.

"Shobha"... Shobha responded with a smile and a handshake.

"You seem to be worried... all okay?" Simran asked with empathy. Shobha just smiled and nodded. She wasn't in any mood to talk. The plane took off in a few minutes. Soon the seatbelt sign was off, and the air hostess started serving refreshments. Simran grabbed her tray while Shobha requested only for a bottle of water. Soon Simran got to her food—a typical Delhi-ite, she was pleased to see 'aloo tikki with chole' in her tray. She didn't waste a minute in taking her first bite. Soon she realized that Shobha was still staring out of the window motionless.

"Are you sure you want to miss out on this scrumptious stuff... it's definitely worth a try," Simran tried to get Shobha talking, but she just smiled in the negative. Food followed some beverages, and both of them requested a cup of tea.

"So we have something in common, we both like tea," Simran made yet another attempt to get talking. Shobha relented this time. Even though she wanted to get out of her somber mood. And soon, both of them started chatting—of course, it was Simran who did most of the talking.

"Official trip? You seem to be worried," Simran asked. Shobha nodded in the negative.

"What about you? Seems you are going home?" Shobha asked.

"I am super excited. You know, I work in Mumbai with a bank and normally go home alternate weekends. But I was never as excited and desperate to land as today," Simran shared her excitement."I can see that, what's special?" Shobha nudged her.

"I am getting married in another four days, just desperate to touch Delhi and rush home. So many things to do – check on final preparations... mehendi the day after... followed by sangeet and then the big grand day on Wednesday... so much to be done and so little time. I haven't even met my friends the last two times I visited Delhi—I was so busy with shopping and preparations," Simran's excitement radiated on her face.

"What about you?" Simran asked, "What's your plan in Delhi?"

"My dad got a stroke late last night and was admitted to the local hospital. He is in ICU," Shobha replied. Simran felt sorry for Shobha and grabbed her hand to make her feel comfortable. Shobha continued in a heavy voice, "I got a call at around 2a.m. Neighbors helped my mom get him to the hospital, and she is all alone there. I just want to get there asap."

"Are you an only child?" Simran asked. Shobha again nodded in the negative. "I have an elder brother who stays in the US. He is boarding a flight in a couple of hours," she added. "He will be all right soon, don't worry," Simran tried to comfort Shobha.

For the next hour or so, Simran tried her best to make Shobha talk. Her objective was to make her feel comfortable and get her out of the pensive mood. In this short trip, they became good friends, exchanged each other's numbers, and hoped for the best for each other. For both of them, the coming three to four days would impact their lives in many ways. Shobha was worried about her father's health and wellbeing. In a contradictory situation, Simran was on her way to embark on a new journey of life. Both sitting next to each other in an opposite frame of mind but equally desperate to land in Delhi. Soon the plane landed, and they went their ways, wishing each other good luck. They both would remember this Wednesday flight from Mumbai to Delhi—met each other as strangers and soon became good friends over a cup of tea 30,000 ft. above.

Fast forward to a busy Tuesday afternoon at Delhi airport. One of the busiest airports, known for its usual hustle-bustle and chaos, with hundreds of flights—domestic and international—taking off daily. At the boarding gate of a flight to Mumbai, two 'known strangers' bumped against each other: Shobha and Simran. "Hi Simran! How are you doing?" Shobha almost screamed with a warm hug. "I am good, hope your father is doing well," Simran asked in a slightly heavy tone. "Yes, he is out of danger and was discharged last evening. All okay," Shobha affirmed. There was a boarding announcement, and both of them joined the queue. As fate would have it, they were seated next to each other—this time Simran in the window seat.

As they boarded the flight, Shobha noticed a significant change in Simran compared to last Wednesday. They settled down in their seats, and Shobha requested water from the cabin crew, offering some to Simran, who accepted it with a short smile. "How is your brother? Has he arrived from the US?" Shobha inquired. "He did, last week," Simran replied. Shobha continued, "We had a couple of tough days last week as Dad was slow to respond to the treatment initially. However, from Thursday, the doctors started getting a positive feeling, and soon things changed. He was out of the ICU in a couple of days, and last evening, they discharged him. He is still not independent but now out of danger. My brother plans to stay for a couple of weeks until things get normal. You know, it was such a relief to see him back, his mere presence was enough to boost me and Mom." Shobha narrated the whole story.

The plane was already in the air, and the seatbelt sign was off. The cabin crew soon started serving refreshments. Shobha grabbed a tray and offered one to Simran, who politely declined. Shobha sensed something was off – Simran was completely different from what she was a week before. "Chole-kulche is worth a try; feel free to grab a bite," Shobha tried to start a conversation again, but Simran just smiled and nodded negatively. Soon, both of them got their cup of tea and started sipping.

"Are you okay, Simran?" Shobha asked. Simran was in tears. Simran was supposed to get married on Saturday, and the fact that she was returning to Mumbai on Tuesday clearly indicated that something was wrong. She was well-dressed but in no way did she look like a newly-wedded bride. "What happened, Simran?"

Shobha grabbed her hand and tried to make her feel comfortable.

"The wedding was called off!" Simran said, and she was immediately in tears. Shobha had a big 'why' on her face but chose not to ask. She knew it was important for Simran to speak on her own. After a couple of minutes, Simran calmed down and cleared her throat. "Manjeet didn't want to marry. They sent a message on Wednesday evening. He didn't even bother to call me and explain!" Simran was visibly anguished. "All preparations, wedding cards, invitations, everything went down the drain. Relatives had already started coming in, and it was such an embarrassment."

Shobha held her hand tightly and kept quiet. She wanted Simran to spill out all the anger and frustration. For the next few minutes, Simran talked about how things unfolded last week and how the family was in deep shock due to Manjeet's decision. It came as a blow, especially to her parents, who were as excited as Simran. However, Simran's father soon gathered courage and decided to move on. Before breakfast on Thursday, he walked up to Simran, who had been crying the whole night. He grabbed both her hands and said, "Manjeet didn't deserve good things in life or probably you deserve much more, don't worry; the family is with you, and we will always be beside you." Simran cried on her father's shoulders for a few minutes and then resolved to move on. Over the weekend, the family decided to get back to normal life as usual, and Simran planned to move back to Mumbai and resume her work.

Shobha patiently listened to Simran's gloomy story, recalling the bubbly and chirpy Simran she met a week back—excited about her life and looking forward to embarking on a new journey. And then, suddenly, things took a sad turn. Shobha held Simran's hand tightly and said, "You know what, we have something in common." Simran looked surprised. "We have a very strong family bond that helps us sail through all the problems in life. My father had a stroke, and the whole family united in no time. We were out of the woods soon. Your family has also stood by your side, and you are almost out of this whole episode." Simran agreed. "Probably, Manjeet didn't deserve the best, or maybe something really great is waiting for you." Both smiled as the plane prepared for landing.

Two flights, the same route, the same passengers on two different days, two exactly opposite states of mind. Life is very tricky in this sense, and you never know when it will turn for the better or worse. But as long as you have a good support system, it doesn't matter.

The Dark Side of Pandemic

SATYAJIT JADHAV, SATHYABHAU AS he was popularly known, retired in January 2020 after a long service as a schoolteacher in the government school. As a respected figure in the village, he was known to everyone. His dedication to society and service was evident with many successful students in the corporate world, some of whom were well settled abroad. Occasionally, some of these students showed their gratitude by visiting him to touch his feet and take blessings.

Sathyabhau was recognized as a very respectable school teacher in the village. He recently retired after a long inning in State Government service with a few trophies for his accomplishments. His elder son was employed in the District Collector's office, and his daughter married to an educated young man in the neighboring village. The younger son had just completed his graduation and was aspiring to pursue further studies. His four-year-old granddaughter was now very happy as she could get most of his time during the day and play all possible tricks with her grandfather. In short, Sathyabhau was leading a full life – a pensioner with an exemplary record in service and a family anyone would be envious of. In society's view, he had successfully completed all his duties as a teacher, as the 'man of the house,' and now as a grandfather. The domestic dog, Moti, was now happy to get more attention and time.

Kansai was a sleepy village in the interiors of Maharashtra. Agriculture was the primary source of employment in the village. Like many Indian villages, Kansai had seen a spate of development activities in recent times – the muddy 'kuccha sadak' was replaced by permanent asphalt 'pukka sadak,' water connections in every house, toilets, solar street lights, bus connections to the nearby town were a few to name. But that didn't change the strong social bonding amongst the villagers. Evenings were pleasant with elders sitting near the central square 'chaupal,' sipping cups of tea, and discussing everything under the sun. But these days, their conversation had a very worrisome topic – the corona pandemic or Covid-19. Starting in far-off China way back in December, the disease was not even known to the village till the prime minister addressed the nation in March. A series of measures being taken by the government was yet to hit the village, but some experienced long-sighted elders like Sathyabhau could sense a bit of impact. Talks of lockdown and movement restrictions took the village by surprise. While the village was self-sufficient, villagers often made trips to the nearby town market to sell fruits and vegetables and earn their livelihood. All this was now tapering off, and movements were getting restricted. Soon, offices in the nearby towns and cities started shutting down, and the nation saw 'reverse migration' of people, especially those who had migrated to greener pastures for livelihood.

Kansai was largely cut off from the world. Its self-sufficient nature helped the village to keep the pandemic at bay. Interaction with the outside world is reduced. A couple of NGOs picked up vegetables and fruits from the village and sold them in cities, thereby easing life for villagers. While the income was reduced, the villagers were happy to avoid traveling to the nearby town. Round-the-clock coverage of Covid-19 news on local channels ensured enough fear among the villagers. Covid-19 now dominated the evening discussions at the chaupal, and everyone was anxious. The only exception was children, who had a great time playing as the schools were closed.

A month passed by, and the village was getting used to the 'new normal'. The Covid infections and victim numbers were increasing day by day across the country. People were getting paranoid and mostly avoided stepping out of the village. The senior citizens continued to meet at the chaupal each evening, but 'social distancing' was a new habit being inculcated. Life was going on, and people were getting used to it.

In early May, the government started facilitating the movement of migrants to their hometowns. This led to a big movement of people from big cities to smaller towns and villages. The movement across districts and states, which was restricted for almost six weeks, was soon allowed. Many factories and companies, in the meanwhile, had either suspended their operations or reduced manpower. People, therefore, preferred to move to their near and dear ones. Like many villages in India, Kansai also saw one of its sons return back. Rajesh Dinkar, aka Raju, was a brilliant boy of the village. He completed his graduation in Pune the year before and had a good job in a local company manufacturing automobile parts. Since there was a temporary suspension of operations, Raju preferred to return to the village and oversee his small piece of agricultural land. Initially, the village was skeptical of his return, but he seemed hale and hearty with absolutely no symptoms of Corona. Also, he chose to confine himself to a limited world to ensure sufficient distance.

A week after his return, Raju stepped out of his house to visit his farm. He happened to meet Sathyabhau on the way and as a routine practice amongst most young men in the village, he immediately touched his feet. Sathyabhau also immediately blessed him with his warm hands and tapped his shoulders. Sathyabhau's mentoring and guidance ensured that the son of a poor uneducated farm laborer completed his education amidst all the challenges and now had a good, stable job. They exchanged a few greetings and headed for their respective destinations.

A couple of days later, Sathyabhau woke up with a sore throat. It did not seem unusual, and Sathyabhau chose to stay at home that day and embraced his home remedies such as drinking hot water, having homemade kadha (a mixture of a few spices and herbs boiled in water) along with light food. Things, however, didn't improve, and he woke up the next day with a mild fever. This further restricted his movement inside his room, and he depended on some known medicines. Kansai was a small village with no medical facilities. The nearest doctor was in the neighboring village about four kilometers, so often people avoided visiting the doctor unless it was inevitable. Cough, cold, fever were considered routine in the village, and often villagers avoided traveling the distance to visit the primary healthcare center.

As there was no sign of improvement, it was decided to call the doctor. By noon, the doctor from the healthcare center visited Sathyabhau. He inspected Sathyabhau's parameters and also studied his symptoms. After administering a small injection, he stepped out of the room, visibly worried and confused. He then made a phone call before returning to talk to Sathyabhau's son. The doctor indicated that he suspected Corona as the symptoms pointed to the possible infection.

Everyone was worried. How? His family members wanted to refute this suspicion since Sathyabhau was at the forefront of educating the villagers about Corona and was very careful. He hasn't stepped out of the village since his retirement a few months back. The possibility could be that he got in touch with some 'covid carrier'. Nobody in the village showed any symptoms of illness, but then Corona was known to be deceiving people with 'asymptomatic carriers'. Was it Raju?

The doctor had called the district hospital, and they had assured to send the ambulance to pick Sathyabhau as soon as possible. However, given the situation across the district and the limited resources, it could be difficult for them to pick him up before evening. The doctor immediately started the preliminary treatment and asked the family to wait for him to be admitted to the hospital.

The news spread across the village like wildfire, and things changed immediately. The village wore a pensive mood. Everyone was talking about him, but nobody wanted to visit him. The grocery shop owner who was supposed to deliver stuff in the afternoon now refused to visit that area. People chose to avoid that route for movement and rather take a roundabout. Things weren't different at home. His family virtually disowned him. A small bed was made outside the house in the garden for him. He was asked to shift there, and his room was locked. A small jug of water was kept on a table next to his bed. Nobody wanted to get close to him, except for two members of the family; the granddaughter wanted to sit next to him because he would always sit next to her when she was sick. She was crying to get to him, but her mother held her back. The other member of the family, who was allowed to be next to Sathyabhau, was Moti, the domestic dog who was with him since birth.

The ambulance arrived from the district hospital in the evening. The ambulance driver along with his companion stepped out with a stretcher and walked towards Sathyabhau. They helped him on the stretcher and started walking towards the ambulance. Sathyabhau looked at the window. His family members were all at the window, the son was in tears, and the daughter-in-law was equally upset. His granddaughter was crying at the top of her voice wanting to embrace her grandfather before he could be pushed on board the ambulance, but she was held back. Sathyabhau just waved his hand. The entire family was in tears and worried about his well-being. The only family member next to him was Moti; he ran after the ambulance to the village limits, not willing to give up.

The ambulance started its journey to the district hospital passing through the village. It crossed the chaupal on its way, and it had an almost full attendance except for its regular prominent member. All the villagers were out of their houses to see the ambulance take Sathyabhau to the hospital. As much as everyone wanted to talk to him and wish him good luck, nobody had the courage to come even closer. It seemed as if they were happy that it wasn't them! Sathyabhau could peep outside the window and wave to the villagers. He could see people worried and sorry for him.

The ambulance finally reached the hospital, and Sathyabhau was formally admitted to the covid ward. It was a small, corner bed in a dimly lit room. He could see a few more patients in a big room. Beds were spaced away from each other to ensure sufficient distance, but that also created a barrier for people to talk amongst themselves. For someone talkative and super active like Sathyabhau, this got claustrophobic in minutes. He could, however, sense the warmth in the health workers who were more than accommodating. They comforted him with a good pep-talk on how patients across the country were recovering fast and India perhaps had the highest recovery rate from Covid.

A brief discussion with the doctor was followed by a simple dinner. Nothing was wrong with the dinner in general, but the real taste was missing. He remembered how his granddaughter would sit next to him and pick up a piece of salad or papad from his plate. The warmth of a family dinner with everyone sitting on the floor in the living room watching the television or discussing something. He couldn't forget Moti, who would sit outside the veranda waiting for Sathyabhau to finish his dinner and then feed him lovingly. Everything changed, and he could feel every pinch now. In the meanwhile, the hospital confirmed the admission to family members, so they were relieved that he was now in safe hands and on the way to recovery. They had their dinner and tried to comfort themselves. Moti sat outside as if he was waiting for the arrival.

Days passed by, and Sathyabhau was getting used to a new routine – simple breakfast, lunch, and dinner. It also included a few cups of tea during the day, regular medicines, and an occasional visit and talk with the doctor. This was very different from his routine for decades. As an early riser, he would get up and go for a long walk with Moti and meet a few villagers on the way. He was missing everything, his morning tea, morning walk, the newspaper, discussions in the Panchayat office, etc. He was now confined to a three-by-six bed with a rather unclean mattress and a pillow. It was difficult for anyone to adjust, but hope kept him going.

The Covid situation was escalating out of control across the country as the number of infected people increased each day. Recovery rates were phenomenal, but not everyone was fortunate. Senior citizens and patients with pre-existing medical conditions were vulnerable. The Covid ward in the hospital had a grim look. Each day witnessed five to six new admissions but also a couple of deaths. It was horrifying, to say the least. Unfortunately, Sathyabhau's condition wasn't improving. Cough and fever didn't subside despite all possible medical care. For him, it was like staring at a dim lamp whose light decreased every minute, and he was facing relentless coughing.

Then came the call from the hospital informing his son that Sathyabhau had finally lost the battle. He succumbed to the pandemic. The family was asked to visit the hospital and pay their last respects if they wanted to. The son broke down, and the news spread in the village within minutes. Almost the whole village gathered at their home and consoled the family. However, nobody in the village was willing to visit the hospital and see Sathyabhau for one last time. The fear of getting infected superseded all the other feelings of respect and love. In fact, the village elders convinced Sathyabhau's son not to visit the hospital in the interest of his family and the village. Unwilling, but finally, the son relented and informed the hospital of their inability to visit him. Finally, the hospital followed the procedure and set for mass cremation along with other deaths for the day.

Sathyabhau was set for his ultimate journey, all alone. Someone who was always surrounded by people was alone in his last journey of life. Someone who had never missed a funeral in the village and who accompanied every family in their days of grief had been left alone today. The pandemic and the eventual fear of death ensured that the village and his family took a step back. A mentor to many young men in the village suddenly saw all his mentees develop cold feet. This is life. You don't know what is in store for you.

Unswerving

SHE WAS EXTREMELY NERVOUS, yet a bit excited as Mugdha walked up to the office of the Chief Executive Officer. She had been with the company for almost eight years and had risen through the ranks. Everyone in the organization would know her personally, and normally, she would make it a point to greet everyone as she passed by their cubicles. However, today was a different day – last evening, the secretary of the CEO called her and requested her to be in the office by 10 am, as the CEO would want to talk to her in person. She knew what it was and had answers to all the questions but was just a bit nervous to face such a strong charismatic person. Finally, she stepped into the CEO's office at 10:00 am sharp. The CEO was amidst some emails but immediately closed his laptop on spotting her. His stern look made her all the more nervous, but he tried to make her comfortable by offering her a seat on the sofa next to his desk.

"I can't imagine" the CEO said while settling down on the sofa and offering a cup of tea to Mugdha. "You were doing so well and were appreciated all along. Your commitment to the organization has been beyond doubt, and you have been doing a fabulous job. You got all the support all the while, and we have always been with you. What has changed now?" A surprised CEO asked Mugdha, who had resigned a day before from her post of Chief Marketing Officer. One of the front faces of the organization for the last few years, Mugdha was a known leader in the company and a motivation to scores of young girls aspiring to make a career in the demanding corporate world.

"Mugdha, I know you personally, and we have been great friends beyond our office commitments. Would you give me the right to ask you what the driver of your decision is?" asked the CEO. With a deep breath and a signature smile, Mugdha replied, "I have a personal commitment, I need to take a step back." Mugdha knew the conversation would go on for long. Many in the organization loved her so much that they couldn't digest her decision, and she was prepared for such conversations. A short pause, and both of them gulped their tea before the CEO asked again, "What can I do to help you reverse your decision?" Mugdha looked at him with a smile and a feeling of acknowledgement but nodded in the negative.

There was silence for a few seconds, and then Mugdha said, "I am planning to go back to my village." The CEO was stunned to hear this. "Really? Are you saying you want to leave Delhi and go to a village which is at least 5 hours drive from the nearest airport? Are you sure you will be able to survive away from the hustle and bustle of a metro?" The CEO was visibly unconvinced. "You can be frank with me, Mugdha. I am all ears," he added.

"It's a very long story," Mugda said. "I made a commitment to someone a few years back, and it's time for me to fulfill my word."

"I am listening," the CEO said with an interest in knowing more.

"You know, I was born and brought up in a small village, Sanad. That's the most wonderful place I had ever seen. Lush green fields, streams of water throughout the year, narrow lanes, clusters of small houses. I can go on. I can still recollect every small corner of the village. The school, the temple, the small shops in the center, the gram panchayat office which was the center of all the activities during the day and also in the evenings. It was simply wonderful. I completed my primary schooling in the village school and then moved to secondary school in the neighboring village. Every day we would walk three kilometers to reach the school. Some days we were lucky to get a lift in the horse-cart, but that's when we were lucky. Two of us – myself and Rajendra – the whole village called him Raj. Both of us belonged to the same community and our parents were good friends."

"Life in the village was very different," Mugdha continued. "We would start the day very early, and the men would head to the farms after a quick bite. The women would finish the work at home and join the men some time later. Children were largely on their own – we would dress up on time and walk to the school, and after coming back, we would just play with friends. No pressure to perform, nobody asked us our grades, no competition- just learn as much as you can and enjoy what you want to. I can't forget the hours

I have spent with my friends in the fields, along the streams and in the village playground. We had only one restriction – return home before sunset. And we never breached that line."

"Raj was very special. Apart from being my classmate, we shared very close family ties. His father had a farm next to ours, so our families were together in good times and bad. I had many friends in the village, and we would play together, study together, pluck mangoes and run when sighted. Raj was with me every moment. Even if he was unwell, he would walk up to the school just to accompany me. He would join me in every activity even if it wasn't sane. I always knew, if I had one reliable friend to trust blindly, it was Raj." As she narrated the whole story, Mugdha was in a different world. Her childhood was in front of her eyes, and she was staring outside the window.

"Then came the horror, when I was in S.S.C, the village was struck by Plague. Many people lost their lives. The village had a small government dispensary which was overwhelmed by the catastrophe. Almost everyone had to be shifted to the Taluka hospital, and things weren't easy there. I lost both my parents, and the whole world turned upside down within a few days. Almost every good thing suddenly came to a close. My mamaji rushed to the village immediately. He was very close to my mom, his elder sister. Being the only child, I was now alone, but mamaji promised that he won't let me be alone even for a minute. Eventually, he decided to take me with him to the town. So after completing all the religious formalities, it was decided that I would pack up and leave the village and join my mamaji's family. I was now about three hundred kilometers from the village, but it was as if I left myself in the village. Not a single day would I remember the village and the serene life I was blessed with."

"I can never forget my last day in the village. I went to the temple, and Raj joined me. We sat under the tree for almost an hour – I was about to leave the village in an hour, and Raj was sobbing all the while. I held his hands together and promised him that I would come back to the village one day. He promised to wait for that day. The whole village came to see me off. The village-head held me tightly with tears in his eyes and kissed my forehead. Everyone in the village was grief-stricken, but they all knew that this was the best decision. Raj ran after our car till the limits of the village, and I kept looking at him till I could see him."

"Life changed for me completely. I was now a part of a new family, and I must say that I was extremely lucky to be accepted and loved here as well. My younger cousin and I gelled well, and in a few days, I got tuned to the new style of living. I joined the local college and resumed my studies. Life in the town was completely different – it was a competition all around: competition for marks, pressure to be accepted in your friend circle-a race to carry yourself better. Initially, I felt very lost, but my younger sister helped me settle down. Soon I adjusted to the new fashionable competitive way of life, but every evening I would sit alone and remember my village. I missed Raj, and I was sure he missed me as well."

"Time flies, I graduated from college and one day saw the advertisement in the newspaper for a possible job in Delhi. I tried my luck and got selected. That's how I landed up in the company. Delhi was a completely different experience compared to my earlier life, but now I have learnt to adapt and move on. I soon picked up the finer tricks of surviving in a metro and worked hard for the last eight years to see myself grow with our company. I must say the company made me successful with the right opportunities, support and guidance. However, even today, every evening I go back to my village, my people, my roots"

"In a couple of months, it will be fifteen years since I left my village. During these fifteen years, a lot has changed for me, and I am sure it has changed for the village as well. I feel now it's time for me to go back to my village. I want to live that life again" A short pause to complete the whole story, and the CEO now realized that it might not be easy to convince Mugdha otherwise. "When was the last time you met Raj?" he asked. Mugdha had a short smile on her face. "It was that last day in the village about fifteen years back. Not since then." "Are you sure you want to leave the job? Why don't you take a few days break, spend some time in the village and see if you want to decide then?" the CEO insisted. Mugdha was undeterred. "I have decided. I am going back. I know Raj is waiting for me, it's time to reunite." The conversation concluded, and the

CEO realized that Mugdha, as always she has been, is firm on her decision.

Soon, Mugdha was out of the corporate world and headed straight to Sanad. It was a long journey from Delhi, but the excitement ensured that it wasn't a tiring one. By late afternoon, she reached Sanad. A lot had changed, and a lot hadn't. The village now had a slightly wider and paved road, but the lush green landscape was the same. Fields on both sides of the road and the stream filled with water were exactly as it was fifteen years back. But the school seemed to have changed, and now it was a bigger one. The shops near the center of the village had grown in size. Mugdha stopped her car in front of her favorite grocery shop – "Banwari chacha." The shopkeeper looked at her and within a few seconds recognized her. "Mugdha" His eyes were filled with tears, he hugged her, kissed her forehead. "I can't believe you are back, he has won," Banwari chacha said. "Who?" Mugdha asked, "Raj, he was the only one in the whole village who was sure that you would come back one day." The two sat down outside the shop, and Banwari chacha continued "after you left, his father promised to take care of your land and house. The gram panchayat transferred the property in your name, and Raj's father was the custodian. Raj has now taken over from his father. He manages your farm as well. Your house, your garden, everything is well maintained. Everyone thought he was mad, but he was sure that one day you would come back." Mugdha was in full tears, "where is he?" she asked "he may have gone to the collector's office in the town. He is now a big man, we elected him as the village head last year, and he takes care of the entire village." Mugdha wanted to hear more, but Banwari chacha insisted that she visit her house, and he promised to send someone to help her clean and cook.

Mugdha reached her house – it was just as it was when she left. Clean, well-maintained and waiting for her. Everything was where it was fifteen years back. Soon, a couple of villagers came to help her settle down and cook something. Mugdha understood that Raj was as committed to her as she was to him – neither of them had forgotten a single word of their discussion in the temple more than a decade ago. The maid gave her a cup of tea – Mugdha smiled and said, "You know what, today I have made the best decision of my life. I am now back to life."

The City of Dreams

MUMBAI, KNOWN AS THE City of Dreams, is the financial capital of the country and the powerhouse for commerce and industry. From the stock exchange to the textile mills, from the film industry to shipping, every industry has a footprint in Mumbai. Known to be amongst the first of the truly cosmopolitan cities in the country, Mumbai has supported the dreams and aspirations of millions. The city is unique in a way – if you have a dream and a will to work hard, there is little chance of your failure. It's a city known for success and rewards.

But life in Mumbai also has a dark side or rather many dark sides. The city runs at a very fast pace, and if you can't cope, you just get lost amidst things. You will know many people around you, but all of them are running in different directions with little time to spare for you. Space has always been a problem in this city, and houses are small. If you compare Mumbai with any other city or smaller town in the country, the quality of life in Mumbai is very poor.

Reshma realized this almost immediately on reaching Mumbai. She had been to Mumbai before, but this time, it was slightly different. She was married to Madhav a few days back and was now a resident of this city. Reshma hailed from Kolhapur – an agricultural town almost 350 kilometers from Mumbai. Her father was a sugarcane farmer and owned a large piece of land. Her elder brother, uncle and cousins helped her father in farming. They were well-to-do, staying as a joint family just outside the city. A big house surrounded by a large garden and trees, a small well in the corner, a couple of pet dogs, two cars and three bikes. That was in complete contrast to her new home – just about 300 sq. ft. small house for a family of four. Her mother-in-law and brother-in-law stayed with them in this small house.

Ram Nivas, the chawl in which Reshma and Madhav stayed, was a house for 40 families. It was a very lively place right at the heart of the city. In the erstwhile days of the seventies and eighties, Mumbai was known for textile mills and was roaring with industrial activities. Like most others in the building, Madhav's father was employed in one such textile mill at a stone-throwing distance from Ram Nivas. Almost everyone staying in the building had been staying together for decades, and in that sense, it was a 'big happy family'. They all welcomed Reshma with open arms, and she soon realized the real warmth of the people.

However, life in the city came with a big cultural shock for Reshma. A smaller house made her feel claustrophobic. Chawls in Mumbai shared toilets, and that made Reshma extremely uncomfortable. The door of the house was always open, and anyone would peep in and talk for a few mins before heading out. Running water for just two hours a day was in sharp contrast to twenty-four hours of running water in Kolhapur. Everyone got up as early as five am, and people headed to their workplaces by around seven to seven-thirty am just to return late in the night. Almost everything in the Mumbai routine was different from her hometown, and she was struggling to cope with that.

But there was one thing that was 'perfect,' Madhav. He was born in Ram Nivas and studied in the local school. His mother was very passionate about getting her sons educated, and that was reflected in his school grades. He was known as one of the brightest kids in the building and appreciated by everyone. He went on to complete his engineering from a local institute and was soon offered a job in a very reputed company in the city. Good job, good salary, and above all, great friends. Madhav's childhood friends in the building were one of his biggest bonds in the building.

Things soon started changing in Mumbai in the nineties. The textile mills were mostly shut down. Most of the factories started setting up their facilities in the outskirts or in another city. The liberalization initiatives by the government brought a new wave of growth, but this time it was for the 'services industry'. The textile mills were soon making way for big commercial complexes and malls. As in the past, the city was running at a very fast pace, and many tried to cope with the pace and did well for themselves, but those who couldn't and started to perish. Crimes in the city started growing, and that was making the residents feel unpleasant.

Then there was a sudden twist in the tale. One morning, Madhav's mother got a letter from the mill that employed his father. The mill owner was planning to sell the land in the prime city center for redevelopment into a commercial center. As a part of the plan, the mill owners wanted to settle all the financial dues of the workers who were abruptly rendered jobless due to the shutdown of its operations in the 1980s. They wanted his mother to personally sign some documents and in return, she was entitled to a hefty pay-out. The mill was abruptly shut down in the 1980s leaving the families of all the workers in limbo. Many like Madhav's father had resorted to small-time jobs to feed the family. He had died a few years ago, but Madhav and his brother remembered every bit of his hard work and struggle to ensure a smooth life for the family. Possibly, this was the beginning of a new phase.

Soon, the formalities were completed, and as promised, the mill owners settled all the financial dues for Madhav's father. Madhav's mother decided to distribute this money equally amongst the two brothers. They decided to purchase two flats in the suburban area of Mumbai and move out of Ram Nivas. Things were changing in

Mumbai – there was a new trend of residential complexes made of multi-storeyed buildings with a lot of amenities. Soon, the two brothers moved into one such community and started a new life. Things were getting slightly better for Reshma now. From a small 300 sq. ft house, she moved to a 900 sq. ft. self-contained flat with all modern facilities. She now got her much-needed sense of privacy and personal space. Madhav also carried on with his professional commitments. He had a busy routine during the week but during the weekend, he would often miss his friends in Ram Nivas. Occasionally, he would visit his friends and his old chawl during the weekends. He had chosen not to sell the Ram Nivas house as it occupied a big emotional space in his heart.

Years passed, and Madhav was now blessed with two daughters. His brother also got married and was well settled. Both the brothers were hard-working and committed to their work. Their dedication ensured that they continued to progress in their lives. Madhav now had become a senior executive in his company. His job demanded frequent travel, within and outside the country. He ensured that he spent every possible minute with his family when he was at home. His visits to Ram Nivas had reduced. One day, he got a call from one of his childhood friends in Ram Nivas, and that made him restless. He decided to visit Ram Nivas the very next morning. Reshma very well sensed the anxiety on Madhav's face but she knew it was about someone in Ram Nivas so she decided to let Madhav on his own. After all, it was his first love.

Today Madhav had visited Ram Nivas after years. He was in touch with many of his friends and their families but seldom got time to visit the place. The condition of the building was deteriorating-its color withered off, plaster on the walls had fallen in a few places. Clearly, the building required some maintenance. However, over the last five to seven years, many of the residents had shifted out of the chawl to some other bigger place, just as Madhav, and now the building was reduced to just about ten occupants. One such occupant was Appasaheb. Now, in his sixties, he was once a lively figure in all the celebrations and festivities in the building. He was staying in the building with his wife and had no offspring. Therefore, he would consider every kid in the building as his own and spent time playing and chatting with everyone.

Unfortunately, his wife expired a few months back, and since then Appasaheb was all alone confined to his room. Last night he slipped on the stairs and that led to multiple fractures. The residents helped him on his bed, but they soon realized that he required hospitalization. That's when they reached out to the erstwhile residents of the building for some help, and that's what got Madhav back to Ram Nivas.

Like Madhav, a few other friends had arrived early in the morning, and they soon got an ambulance to move Appasaheb to the nearby hospital. The hospital was one of the finest in the city and was known for state-of-the-art facilities and the quality of treatment. Appasaheb was a lower-middle-class man with meager savings, but the chawl residents didn't agree to his request to move to a local government hospital. Instead, they chose an experienced doctor and agreed on a surgical intervention as suggested by him. Soon, the surgery started, and it was supposed to be a long one. Many residents of the chawl – present and erstwhile – were seen mingling around the operation theater and the waiting area. Madhav met a few of his childhood friends after a few years, and conversations started immediately.

Like him, many of his friends had now stepped out of Ram Nivas. Some relocated to suburban localities for bigger houses, and a few had even moved to other cities. After some initial catch-up and updates, they went down memory lane – the good old childhood days – the way they played and quarreled – the way some of the seniors like Appasaheb intervened and sorted out the fights – the breaks between the games for a sip of juice or snack offered by someone in the building, stories, stories, and only stories. But today, some of them had visited Ram Nivas and saw that it was in a very depleted state. A lively and happening place had now turned into ruins. It seemed like the skeletons were out, and the building was in a poor state. The fact that it was largely unoccupied added to its woes. Incidentally, almost two decades back, Appasaheb had championed the initiative to renovate the building. He not only convinced every resident about the need to repair but also ensured that they all contributed and participated as required. However, now the building was representing Appasaheb's state – old and left to itself.

This thought made Madhav and his friends very restless. They were nurtured and caressed by the residents of this very chawl when they were young. But when they grew up, they felt the need to move out and eventually forgot the great place which was a treasure of their memories. In this rat race to move ahead in life, they missed the very fabric that made them capable of running this race. They felt guilty; some even felt selfish that they didn't care for the ones who cared for them. However, given the situation, they chose to bury the feelings and the subject for now.

Soon, the good news came from the operation theater. The surgery was successful, and Appasaheb was doing well. He was moved to the recovery room, and everyone felt relieved. Madhav and his friends stepped out for a cup of tea at the nearby stall. Madhav then suggested that it was their time to do something for Ram Nivas and its residents — a feeling that was echoed by everyone. They all had come a long way in their lives and were capable of doing something – after all, they continued to own a place in Ram Nivas but more importantly, the building was a witness to their golden phase of life. They left for their homes with a pledge to change things on a priority. Madhav returned home – exhausted and worried. He told Reshma how serious

Appasaheb was and how they had to run around to get him the right treatment. Reshma gave a patient hearing and then said, "You guys did a fabulous job today; you have saved Appasaheb, and soon he will be as independent as he was. What's the worry now?" Madhav then talked about his feelings for Ram Nivas, which she could relate to. She held his hand and said, "I am sure you boys will be able to manage that. Ram Nivas now needs its kids to help, and you should not shy away." She went back to the kitchen, but her supporting words meant a lot to a determined Madhav.

The next morning, the friends met again at the hospital. Appasaheb was now visibly comfortable and recouping. His eyes were full of tears to see how these kids stepped in to save him. After all, he always treated them like his own kids. But this was beyond his expectation – the boys not only came at the right time but also made some good decisions for him as if he was a part of their family. They contributed to the entire hospital expense and ensured that he didn't feel any burden. Later, the boys again went to the tea stall, this time to make some decisions. They had now decided to renovate and repair Ram Nivas. One of them was a civil contractor himself, and they decided to entrust him with all the responsibilities. They also decided to contribute the lion's share of the costs to ensure a lesser impact on the less privileged members of the building. The work started almost immediately, and most of them participated wholeheartedly.

In a couple of months' time, Ram Nivas was ready to host a party for all its residents. The renovation was all done, and now it had a much younger and lively look. All the residents of the building, including the ones who were now staying elsewhere, met for a get-together. The same pomp-and-show with delicious food and music. It felt as if they had just moved a couple of decades back and it was lively once again. Appasaheb was also recovering fast... he was able to walk albeit with crutches and the satisfaction and happiness on his face were a representation of how Ram Nivas felt.

Reshma had joined this party and she was so fascinated by the excited and happy faces of the residents and erstwhile residents of Ram Nivas. She was wrong to assume that Mumbai was heartless, this incident showed that the residents of the 'maximum city' were as caring and loving as the residents of any other town in the country. It's just that Mumbai has a different pace and often people fail to see the beautiful surroundings in their pursuit to run faster.

Each of His Own

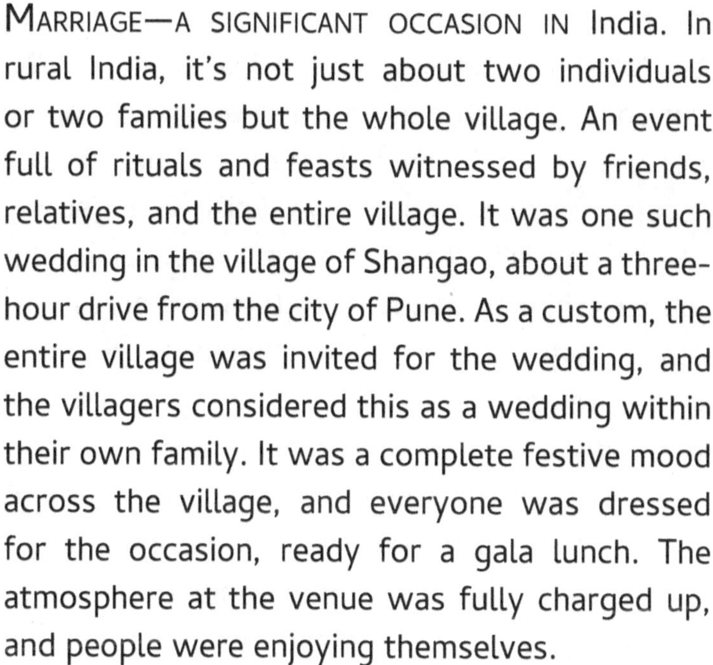

MARRIAGE—A SIGNIFICANT OCCASION IN India. In rural India, it's not just about two individuals or two families but the whole village. An event full of rituals and feasts witnessed by friends, relatives, and the entire village. It was one such wedding in the village of Shangao, about a three-hour drive from the city of Pune. As a custom, the entire village was invited for the wedding, and the villagers considered this as a wedding within their own family. It was a complete festive mood across the village, and everyone was dressed for the occasion, ready for a gala lunch. The atmosphere at the venue was fully charged up, and people were enjoying themselves.

Suddenly, a young man, Sudhir, saw someone and left his group conversation halfway to walk up to another young man. The two stared at each other for a second and then hugged. Sudhir had met his childhood friend, Vishwas, after a long time, and his main purpose for traveling all the way to the village was achieved. Sudhir and

Vishwas studied together in school and were best friends. Sudhir's father was employed in the local Tahsildar's office, whereas Vishwas was a son of a farmer. When they were about to complete their school, Sudhir's father was transferred to Pune, and he moved with his family. Sudhir continued his studies in Pune and went on to become an engineer. Subsequently, he joined a leading software company, which changed his life completely. Apart from a good salary, his job gave him an opportunity to travel across the globe. Vishwas, on the other hand, stayed back in the village. He completed his graduation at the local college and joined his father in farming. The two friends embarked on their own journeys and did well for themselves. In the initial days, Sudhir would visit his grandparents in the village almost every month, and the friends had a good time together. However, after the demise of his grandparents, his visits became less frequent. Moreover, a busy schedule and regular business travel made such visits even more infrequent. It had been a good two years since Sudhir had visited the village, so when he heard about the wedding, he decided that he had to visit and meet his old acquaintances in the village.

The day was busy for the village—marriage rituals followed by lunch went on until late afternoon. In the evening, Sudhir and Vishwas went to their favorite childhood spot—the stream where they spent hours playing in water and climbing trees. They had a lot to catch up on. Sudhir was now a successful software professional managing international clients. He had a spacious flat in Pune. He was married, and his son was scheduled to complete his school this year. Vishwas, on the other hand, was a successful farmer. He had purchased a few more pieces of land in the village and used all the possible modern techniques to increase his yield.

Though he was doing well, it was very evident that Sudhir was miles ahead in his standard of living as well as the quality of life. Vishwas asked curiously if he could explore an opportunity in Pune for himself, and Sudhir was excited. He knew a few people who were in agribusiness, and Vishwas would love to work with them. Soon, Vishwas got a good job in Pune and moved along with his wife and son. Sudhir ensured a good flat for Vishwas in the nearby locality. The two friends were now staying very close. The families would meet twice a month for dinner, and their conversations often lasted until late at night. Vishwas was doing well in his new job, and since it was related to the marketing of agricultural products, he could use all his experience and knowledge.

Months passed by, and the friends continued their successful run in their respective spaces. Vishwas, however, was feeling very restless in the way things were happening for him. Of course, he was thankful to Sudhir for helping him settle down in Pune. He now had a good property and a well-paying job. He was well respected in his company, and his hard work was reciprocated by the company with good remuneration and authority. He was, however, feeling claustrophobic. He was missing his village—the open fields, the stream, the village temple which was the center of all the activities in the village. Though he knew many people here in the city, he saw a lack of warmth in these relationships. He felt the greetings were formal and lacked empathy. He also felt that life was nothing but a routine following the watch. He was making more money, but the family was missing him at the dinner table. Often, he would leave for the office before his son got up, and he really missed talking to him. He soon realized that the city got him good money and opportunity but at a huge cost. As days passed, he was getting increasingly restless.

On a Saturday evening, Sudhir visited Vishwas for dinner. After their regular chats and dinner, the two friends went for a stroll. Sudhir could notice that all was not well with Vishwas. He, therefore, asked Vishwas about his worry. Vishwas opened up with Sudhir. Clearly, he was missing his village and the associated peace of mind there. Sudhir understood his point and asked him if he wanted to revisit his decision. After an hour of discussion, Vishwas made up his mind... he wanted to leave the city and go back to his village. Sudhir was supportive of this decision and helped him in planning a smooth movement.

Soon, Vishwas started winding up. He had left his job, sold his property, got his son a good hostel to continue with his studies, and was all set to move back to the village in the next two weeks. Sudhir was with him all the while and helped him in every possible way. Again, the two friends met over dinner on Saturday. Sudhir was a bit upset, he was going to miss Vishwas. He was so happy a couple of years back when Vishwas moved to the city. The two friends were back to their old days, chatting freely and spending a good time with each other. Now, he was again going to be alone. On the other hand, even he had started feeling a sense of fatigue. He had a tough schedule with no time left for himself or his family. His job gave him immense wealth, but it left him lonely and tired. He was also very keen to move to a more meaningful life. Vishwas asked him a surprise question, "Why not move to the village."

He already had a house in the village. He also had a small farm and had some ideas for organic farming. "Maybe this is the time," Vishwas said. The two friends brainstormed this idea, and Sudhir decided to discuss this with his family before concluding. His family was a bit jittery but was not averse to exploring village life. Soon, Sudhir decided to join Vishwas in their village in the next two to three months. Vishwas moved to the village and got back to what he loved—farming. He also started getting things ready for Sudhir to move to the village. His old house was renovated, and some furniture was changed.

With the help of a few village laborers, he cleaned Sudhir's farm and got it ready for sowing.

Soon, Sudhir moved to the village. He was thrilled to be there. His village house was more than double the space of his city flat. A good garden in front and back of the house ensured enough space for everything in life. He soon started getting used to village life. He loved getting up at his will, rather than a preset alarm. He now had enough time and a garden where he could sip his morning tea. He would spend most of his day on the farm caring for his plants and the produce. He also established a good customer base for his farm output. In the evenings, he would visit the village center and meet a few friends, including Vishwas. He also helped other farmers in the village in establishing a good customer base for their farm produce. Soon, people started loving him for his views and knowledge. He also had enough spare time to visit the village school and teach the computer to the students. He had donated a few books and computers to the school.

Life went on, and Sudhir was getting used to a new life away from the hustle-bustle of the city. It was full of 'me time,' and he could do what he wanted. He could also have a good time with his family. He brought in new concepts to farming and also helped his fellow farmers in the village to gain from his knowledge. It went on for a couple of years, and he seemed to have settled down. However, he soon started getting restless again. The village gave him all the love and respect one would look for. However, it came with its challenges and constraints. To begin with, he was too dependent on his inverter for power, as there were frequent and long power cuts. Like in any typical village, life came to a complete shut down by around eight pm, and even the main center felt isolated by ten pm. The village had a primary health center, but it lacked a full-time doctor. Any emergency and you had to travel about five kilometers for help. The village had a couple of grocery shops, but the exotic stuff that he loved would require a trip of at least ten kilometers. A good restaurant or bar would also mean a long drive. Home delivery of medicines, food, grocery, vegetables, etc., was unheard of, and hardly a few retail chains serviced the village.

Sudhir soon realized that while rural life was peaceful and calm, it came with its own drawbacks. Sudhir spent his childhood in this very village, but since his college days, he was in the city, and slowly he had gotten used to many comforts that are a hallmark of cities. While Sudhir was enjoying his stay in the village, the 'fear of missing out' started kicking in. He was in regular touch with many of his former office colleagues and friends. From their social media posts, he could see how fast the world was moving. Somewhere he felt stuck in the village and was worried that he would soon be left out. He could also see that anxiety in his family.

One fine day, his old boss reached out to him through social media. They were planning to set up a new company in Pune, and he was checking if Sudhir was keen to get back to corporate life. Sudhir didn't spare even a second to say yes and decided to wrap up his set-up in the village and move back to the city. With a heavy heart, Vishwas accepted his decision and helped him in moving back to the city. Sudhir soon resumed his corporate life and was back on track. However, he decided that he would visit the village at least once a quarter for a week or so and ensure that he spent some quality time there.

Life is tricky in some sense. We always feel the other person is blessed and better off. It's only when you go through the cycle that you realize that you are good in your own habitat. No doubt there are challenges and constraints, but there are always ways to be happy within those. To each his own.

The Destiny

IT WAS LATE EVENING, and Kamleshbhai was winding up his long, exhaustive day. Most of his staff members had already left for the day, and he was closing the shutters of his shop. His large shop in the city center was now one of the most famous grocery shops in this small town of Jadhavnagar. The staff handed over the keys of the shop and left while Kamleshbhai was staring at his shop, looking back at his journey.

Until a few years back, Kamleshbhai owned a small stationery shop in the same area. The shop was almost one-fourth the size with just two staff members helping manage the business. He had taken over this shop when his father died a few years ago. Kamleshbhai had grown in this shop and had seen his father toil hard to set up this business. He continued to run this shop and worked very hard to grow the business. However, the nature of the business and the competition in the area made it very difficult for him to grow. However, Kamleshbhai didn't want to accept one truth—that he was never interested in this business. He was managing this shop only in memory of his late father. He always had a very different view of the business. In his view, there were two key elements to success: (i) the business should employ many people, directly or indirectly, and (ii) it should be such that people in far-off villages also benefit from his business acumen. In his view, a grocery shop was closest to his goal. However, he didn't have the courage to choose his passion over his father's reminiscence, so he always avoided any decision.

And then, destiny came calling in early 2020. With Covid-19 fears, businesses started showing a downward trend across the market. Shops were closing down, and people started moving away from investing in their businesses. The number of customers visiting the shop reduced, and so did the income. Distributors on the other hand were pestering for speedy clearance of their credit as they were also worried about their businesses. It was a very gloomy situation. And then came the final blow—the government announced a complete lockdown for a few weeks in March, and all shops were ordered to be closed. The entire nation was in a state of fear; with the markets closed and schools and offices shut down, the nation had come to a standstill. People were afraid to step out for groceries and medicines, so the idea of betting money on the stationery business was off the table. The business was staring at a dead-end, and Kamleshbhai was a worried man.

One evening in early April, Kamleshbhai's mobile rang—it was one of his closest school friends. Kamleshbhai was almost in tears when he was narrating his plight, and then came a sentence that changed his life; his friend said, "This is the time. Bring the change you always wanted to." His friend knew his passion, and he also knew that Kamleshbhai wasn't able to make a decision for long. This was, however, the right time to change. The idea struck him well, but he didn't know how to start, as the time was not right to start anything new. After mulling over the idea for a couple of days, he called Jayantkaka, his father's younger brother. He was a successful businessman in another city and was very close to Kamleshbhai. Jayantkaka knew a grocery merchant close to Jadhavnagar and introduced the two. Kamleshbhai then had a master idea, and things just started moving.

Kamleshbhai had a good network in business circles, as his father was a respected businessman. Through his contacts, he started accepting grocery orders. He would then pick up stuff from the warehouse of his uncle's friend and deliver it to the customers. By then, the government had relaxed a few norms, and movements for essential services were allowed, which meant Kamleshbhai could drive across the town and make deliveries to customers. Everything was going well for him, as this was the kind of business he wanted to own, and the prevailing situation made customers realize the convenience of ordering essentials. In short, Kamleshbhai was able to pursue his passion.

There were two reasons that facilitated the growth of his business: first, groceries were in demand given the pandemic situation, and anyone ready to deliver stuff at home was in high demand; and second and most importantly, it was Kamleshbhai's enthusiasm and passion that ensured that he was on top of all the hurdles. He, however, knew that he would need to come up with innovative ideas if he wanted to grow in his new endeavor. From accepting money in digital modes to accepting orders through various electronic channels, he was open to changing the way the situation demanded. He ensured that he was honest with his customers, and they trusted him. But while growing the business was his priority, he never lost focus on his other objective – to ensure that he provided livelihood to as many people as possible. To begin with, he looked out for a few transport workers who were suddenly unemployed during the lockdown. This proved to be the silver lining for the workers who had otherwise lost all hopes. Not only did he provide them with employment and money, but he also provided them with hope for a better tomorrow. Secondly, through his friends and acquaintances, he reached out to heads of a few villages nearby to see if he could buy grains and vegetables directly from the farmers. This, of course, solved the 'supply chain' problem for him, as he now started getting fresh products directly from villagers. However, in the real sense, he also ensured that he provided a market to the poor farmers who otherwise were amongst the worst hit. In a true sense, he was adding a lot of value to society while building his business. Things just kept moving north. Kamleshbhai continued to grow his network, accepting orders during the day, and delivering stuff before evening. The day was usually exhausting, but he never relented even for a minute. He soon set up a small godown on the outskirts to store and receive his products. The number of employees increased, and so were the activities for the day. Liaising with distributors, farmers, and customers kept him busy the whole day, but it also ensured that he kept growing at a fast pace.

While settling down in his new business, Kamleshbhai thought that it was time to think big. He, therefore, bought the shop next to his stationery shop in the city centre. Of course, he paid a hefty amount, but he never wanted to leave the shop where he started his business. He always wanted to continue with the place where it all started. He soon converted his stationery shop into an expanded grocery shop. However, two things didn't change: his seat in the shop continued to be the same where his father used to sit when he started the shop. Also, the two employees who helped him manage this stationery shop continued to be his employees in the new business as well.

Markets slowly started opening up, and footfalls in the shop increased. People were delighted to see a big grocery shop that was also accepting orders electronically and delivering stuff to their residences. All in all, he had developed a very sound online and offline business model.

Kamleshbhai set an example for many in our society. The pandemic hit everyone alike – businesses were impacted, demand was at a standstill, companies started laying off employees, salaries reduced, and there was a gloomy scenario everywhere. Many people had to wind up their businesses and look for other options. Some wound up their set-up in cities and moved to their hometown in search of cheaper modes to exist.

But there are many 'Kamleshbhais' in our society as well. These are the optimistic members of our society who chose to ignore all the dark clouds around them and continued to work hard. They were not pulled back by circumstances; instead, they chose to use the prevailing situation to their advantage. These are the people who saw something positive for them in every situation and who were willing to go the extra mile to convert every opportunity that they sensed.

But to be successful, apart from a positive attitude, you also need to think about others around you. Alone can only get you so much. For someone to make a bigger mark, it is also important to take society with you. One reason why Kamleshbhai was so successful in such a short time was his intention to help the ones who were hit by the situation. He chose to help people in distress, and they, in turn, ensured that he wasn't let down. People around him helped him with all their vigor to ensure that he didn't fail, and that's what made him really successful.

In short, it is fine to safeguard your interest and pursue your priorities, but never forget the people around you. If you take people along with you, you will surely reach your destiny, and probably reach much faster.

The Rich Poor Man

IT WAS A RAINY Friday evening, and Suman hosted a small party for four of his childhood friends. This reunion of five schoolmates, all in their thirties, was in its full form. They had met after a few years, so they had lots of stories to tell. Each of them was successful in their own right, and everyone wanted to hear about the other. So, the occasion was full of fun, stories, drinks, and food. Suddenly, one of them got a message on a social media website, and the atmosphere took a complete turn. They were visibly restless and desolate. One of them suggested a plan, and others agreed readily. Suman, who was the only teetotaller in the group, grabbed the keys to his car, and the others followed him in his sedan. The group was off to a small village, Vadapa, in the coastal belt of Maharashtra – approximately five hours' drive from Mumbai.

Vadapa was a small village of approximately 2000 families surrounded by a few smaller villages nearby. The area was famous for the rich delicious variety of Alphonso mangoes, and the villagers were very proud of the fruit, which was largely exported. Agriculture being the primary source of employment, most young men would migrate to big cities for jobs post-education. The village had a government-run High School, and kids from the nearby villages would walk up to the school for education. Like many government-run schools, this school also struggled on many counts – the school building was in a poor state, lack of teaching staff and amenities made it difficult for the existing staff members, and rains would almost always be accompanied by waterlogging and leakages. However, the school was known for one strong, robust support system, its headmaster – Gangadhar Sathe, who was popularly known as Masterji. Unfortunately, he had suffered a massive stroke that evening, and the news prompted these five young men to abort their night-out plans and head to Vadapa to take charge of the situation.

Masterji was known to almost every household. He had dedicated his whole life to educating young kids in villages. Almost thirty years back when the government started this school in the village, he had moved to the village as a school teacher and dedicated the rest of his life to the village. Back then, education wasn't the priority for the poor villagers, and the kids spent most of their time playing near the farms. In the next few years, Masterji changed the whole mindset. He used to walk across the village and visit almost every house persuading the parents to send their kids to the school. In many cases, villagers sent their children to school not because they believed in education but because they couldn't say 'no' to Masterji. His passion was for everyone to see.

Soon, all the kids in the village started going to school, but Masterji didn't stop there. He visited many small villages in the nearby area and persuaded those villagers as well. He was, therefore, known to almost everyone in the village and commanded a sense of respect. Village elders and the Panchayat also wholeheartedly supported Masterji in making education a priority for the village. He nurtured this school as his own baby, and villagers could feel his passion and commitment.

After a few years, Masterji got married, and his wife was popularly known as 'Masterniji' in the village. She had no background in teaching but soon got carried away by Masterji's dedication. She started helping him with various administrative tasks. Often, she would visit the nearby town to buy stationery or books for the school and shoulder Masterji's responsibilities. She also helped him in managing the day-to-day affairs of the school. Village schools in those days were surrounded by multiple issues. Lack of infrastructure was the single biggest but not the only issue. There was a daily struggle around basics like drinking water, hygiene, cleanliness, electricity, etc., but the couple did everything they could to move things. Many villagers came from a poor financial background, and it was difficult for them to pay fees and afford books, stationery, etc. Masterji was often seen stepping in by contributing some money or helping with books or stationery. His salary was just about sufficient for his personal needs, but his compassionate wife ensured that he could contribute beyond his means and engage in his mission.

Masterji had a very tough personal life. A small salary was just about sufficient for the couple to meet their ends. To ensure that children of poor villagers didn't drop out of school, Masterji often contributed in multiple ways, including their fees, books, bags, etc. All these social contributions left the family with negligible savings for the future. While Masterniji was very happy to support her husband in his objective, she was always worried about the future. They knew very well that a meager pension post-retirement would be insufficient for the couple to survive. The village was not aloof from the rising cost of living and thereby rising worries for Masterniji. Above all, they were childless, and that was a big grief for Masterniji. This, however, never deterred Masterji, and he continued with his calling. He had just one objective in life – groom the poor children in the village so that they were able to meet the challenges of tomorrow. As if the couple had adopted all the children of the village and nurtured them as their own.

The village only had a Higher Secondary school, which meant that the kids had to travel to the district place for college and higher education. But their hardship was not restricted to only travel and costs. Many children often felt lost when they stepped into the bigger world. Masterji was well aware of these cracks and ensured that they never fell through them.

He would regularly visit their houses and talk to them for a few minutes. His constant pep-talk and guidance ensured that the children continued their journey. Many children from the village picked up higher education and were successful in their lives. Some even pursued specialized professional education and took up good jobs in cities across the country. Masterji was never short of words in talking about such great stars from the village. He could see his mission being successful.

Masterji was always close to the heart of his students. Children completed their Higher Secondary education and left the school, but they never left Masterji. He was always around for them – to talk to them, guide them, understand their problems and suggest some solutions. He was a sound mentor who always helped his mentees sail to success. As they grew up in life, they respected him more and more. They started realizing the hardships that he had faced to ensure that their education was smooth. They appreciated all his contributions, financial and otherwise. Many children knew that their success in life would have been impossible without Masterji.

Masterji had retired a couple of years earlier, but his mission continued. While he had handed over the reign of the school to his successor, the village always regarded him as the Masterji, and he also continued with his good work of ensuring the culture of education continued. Financially, of course, he was feeling the pinch. His small pension was slightly less for the couple to survive, and with old age, medicines and other requirements were hitting them hard. Villagers were very well aware of their hardships and never hesitated to help. Many contributed in their own way by sharing some portions of the vegetables and fruits grown in their fields. The couple was able to meet the ends somehow.

Since Friday morning, Masterji has been feeling a bit uneasy. He was sure everything wasn't normal but thought it was a part of old age issues. He felt slight heaviness on his right part of the body, and his speech was getting blurred. By around three pm, he suffered a massive stroke. Masterni Ji immediately alerted the neighbors, and they called the doctor from the village health center. The doctor was quick to arrive but soon realized that treatment would need hospitalization. Unfortunately, the health center was ill-equipped for such emergencies. Medicines and injections required for this treatment would be available only in the nearby town. He, therefore, suggested that they move Masterji to the municipal hospital at the district place. Soon an ambulance arrived, and Masterji was shifted. Few known people from the village accompanied Masterniji to help her. By evening, Masterji was admitted to the local municipal hospital.

News spread like wildfire. Being a small village, everyone got to know everything in a few minutes. Social media helped convey this message to far-off cities. It was through one such channel that Suman and his friends got to know about the incident while they were partying. The guys had decided to make a quick weekend trip to their native – Vadapa village, which was still a small, sleepy village.

By the early hours of Saturday, they had reached the municipal hospital at the district place. They could see Masterni Ji along with a couple of villagers waiting outside the general ward. She was completely shattered. Masterji was her only support for decades, and she was gripped with fear for his health. As the ritual in the village would go, the five guys immediately touched her feet, and she was very surprised to see them. But this also gave her comfort and support. They had a brief chat, and Masterniji recalled the whole incident from Friday afternoon. The group convinced her that she was not alone and the whole village was with her. The fact that five of Masterji's students rushed all the way from Mumbai was heart-warming. She was, however, worried about the future. While she resisted talking openly, she confided in Suman about their financial situation and was worried about how they would be able to manage their day-to-day expenses with a meager pension. Suman assured her that something would be done before they left for Mumbai.

The doctor visited the ward on Saturday morning, and the group waited eagerly for a briefing. The doctor confirmed that he was responding to medicines but he wasn't completely out of danger. It wasn't very pleasant news. The five guys stepped out of the hospital for a quick breakfast but were in a somber mood. One of them suggested that they move Masterji to a specialty hospital nearby, and they agreed unanimously. Soon, they returned to the hospital to share their views with Masterniji. While her immediate reaction was affirmative, she soon took a step back. A specialty hospital would cost loads of money, and she wasn't prepared for it. Suman soon realized the reason for her hesitance and assured her that everything would be taken care of. Her eyes filled with tears when she agreed to the plan. Soon, the group worked out the logistics and before noon, Masterji was moved to a private hospital that specialized in the treatment of a stroke. Suman had swiped his credit card to take care of the entire hospital expenses, and the others had agreed to share the cost.

Soon, the news spread that Suman and his friends had moved Masterji to a private hospital. Villagers were happy, more so because a group of his students remembered Masterji and his contribution to their lives. Masterji had shaped their future by molding them in the tender years, and they didn't forget all the good deeds done to them. Social media groups were abuzz with the news. More and more students now wanted to support in whichever way they could. Suman had an idea. Knowing the financial situation that

Masterji was in, he suggested everyone transfer whatever they could to Masterniji's bank account. Suman shared her account with the group and requested them to contribute whatever possible, even if it was a small amount.

The group again visited the hospital on Sunday morning. Masterji was doing well now. The doctors indicated that he was now out of danger and could go home in another two to three days. That was a big sigh of relief for everyone. The group also met Masterji, he was conscious and immediately recognized his students. Both Masterji and his wife were in tears. They sacrificed their whole life for the education of the village children but never thought that they had actually made the best investment in life. They never imagined that their selfless hard work for society would pay off so well. Soon, they all left the hospital and let Masterji rest.

By the time it was afternoon, Masterniji's bank account was flooded with contributions. She now had almost Rs. 10 lac contributed by many of their former students. Suman had promised her last night that 'everything will be taken care of" and he did what he said. In their lifetime, they had never seen so much money. Late afternoon, Suman and his friends visited the hospital again. They were heading back to Mumbai and wanted to meet Masterniji before heading back. She was now free of her worries – Masterji was out of danger and would be back home soon. Moreover, they were no longer in financial distress. Suman had ensured that they had enough for them to lead a cozy life back home. Masterji led a simple life and he managed all his expenses, including the ones that he incurred for poor students in the village, all within a small government salary. However, he made some very sound investments in life—investment in children, investment of effort, passion, and everything he could. That investment was now blossoming up, and he was no longer a poor man.

Life After Death

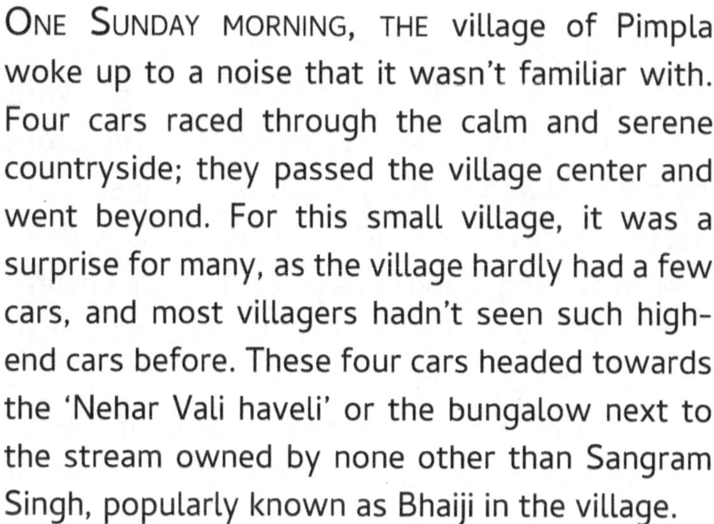

One Sunday morning, the village of Pimpla woke up to a noise that it wasn't familiar with. Four cars raced through the calm and serene countryside; they passed the village center and went beyond. For this small village, it was a surprise for many, as the village hardly had a few cars, and most villagers hadn't seen such high-end cars before. These four cars headed towards the 'Nehar Vali haveli' or the bungalow next to the stream owned by none other than Sangram Singh, popularly known as Bhaiji in the village.

Bhaiji was the richest landlord in the area. He owned almost half of the cultivable land in Pimpla village, and many people from the village were employed in his farms. He had a huge bungalow overlooking the stream, giving it the name 'Nehar Vali haveli'. Bhaiji lost his father when he was fifteen years old. As he was the only son, he was forced to plunge into his father's shoes, and soon he left his school. His mother was a great influence on him, and she molded him into a great human being. Though Bhaiji left school midway, he never left his education; his mother ensured that he read and studied aspects that were important to be a great human being.

Bhaiji got married in his early twenties and embarked on a blissful married life. His wife, Sumadevi, was a perfect companion who stood by her husband in every situation. Very soon, he settled well in both his journeys. He was doing well in farming; good rains year after year ensured good crops, which in turn resulted in good money. Instead of spending money on himself, he used this to occasionally add small pieces of land to his already big estate. On the family front, he was blessed with three sons. He seemed to be on top of the world. However, despite being rich and mighty, he led a very modest lifestyle.

Time passed by. Over a period, he owned almost half of the village land and was well recognized and respected in the surrounding areas. He bought a piece of land next to a stream and constructed a big house for the family. Due to its location, it was referred to as 'Nehar Wali haveli' by the villagers. He employed many people in his farms who helped him in the day-to-day work. He ensured that his laborers were taken care of. Even during hard days of famine, the laborers didn't go hungry. He also helped his laborers financially during festivals or for any unexpected event. For an outsider, Bhaiji led a 'textbook perfect' life — a perfect family, enormous wealth, loads of respect, and an envious lifestyle.

Years passed by, and his children soon stepped out of the village. Initially, for studies and later for work, the children spent most of their time in cities and visited the village only on occasions or holidays. For the villagers, Bhaiji had an ideal life, but he himself knew that there was something imperfect. These imperfections only kept on increasing as the days passed. Bhaiji was known to be a 'down-to-earth' and simple man who was always accessible and helpful. However, his sons slightly drifted away with ego. The feeling of belonging to a rich and powerful family often pushed them away from basic etiquettes. They were far from polite and picked up fights over small issues. The villagers knew them as rude and disrespectful children. Bhaiji saw all this and often reprimanded them. However, things only moved in the wrong direction.

As the children grew, Bhaiji started growing nervous. He always wanted at least one of his sons to continue with his passion for farming and help the villagers during the bad times. His sons, on the other hand, wanted to be a part of the family prestige and wealth but didn't share the values and morals. They wanted the village to bow down to them but never learned the trick of gaining admiration.

After completing their education, they stepped into the corporate world and moved to big cities to pursue a career. Normally, they would come home for important festivals like Diwali and Holi. As time passed by, their visits to the village were less frequent and short. In the earlier days, they would stay back for at least a week but later started making shorter trips. Bhaiji started feeling that his sons were distancing themselves from their village.

The eldest son got married a few years ago to one of his college mates. Despite social and economic gaps between the families, Bhaiji readily approved the marriage. He was keen that his son married a girl of his choice and committed himself to a long and blissful relationship. Bhaiji wanted the first marriage in the family to take place in the village. He wanted to host a feast for the entire village. His son, however, had other plans. He was planning a lavish wedding in a reputed hotel in the city. In the interest of his son's happiness, Bhaiji agreed.

Inviting the whole village to the city for a wedding, that too in a posh reputed hotel, was not a good idea. Apart from being very expensive, the villagers would find themselves out of place and perplexed. He, therefore, decided to host a lavish dinner for all his acquaintances a day after the wedding. His son and daughter-in-law visited the village and graced the occasion but didn't stay for long. Very soon his second son also got married. It was a low-key affair with very few friends and relatives. The wedding was in a banquet hall in a city miles away from the village. This time, there wasn't a lavish feast for the village, but only a few sweets to the employees.

By now, the villagers had realized that Bhaiji's sons had distanced themselves from the village. They were so much happier in their city life that they forgot the village and its people. Some elders in the village had foreseen this and had warned Bhaiji a decade back, but he wasn't ready to believe them.

Time passed, and Bhaiji was growing old. Age-related ailments started affecting him. His stamina reduced, and so did his ability to work hard and long hours in the fields. He and his wife spent most of their time at home together. They would talk about all the good things in life, how they got married at a young age, how they built a big house, their sons, their education, marriage, etc. However, his sons were not concerned about them. Except for an occasional phone call or a once-in-a-while visit to the village, the sons were busy in their own lives.

Bhaiji and his wife started feeling lonely and isolated. Such a big house, built to accommodate a big joint family with many children, was now occupied only by an old couple and a few of their servants. Some of his trusted employees were always with them all the while. So much so that when he had a heart attack, the villagers took him to the town and ensured that he was admitted for the best treatment. Sumadevi was next to him every minute, but his two elder sons visited him in the hospital a couple of days later.

His youngest son couldn't find time to travel all the way to the village; he just called his mother a couple of times and inquired about his health.

Soon, Bhaiji was back at home. Timely and proper treatment ensured that he was safe and recovering. However, he was now convinced that he couldn't depend on his sons to take care of him or his wife in the final days. He was more worried about his wife should anything happen to him. Almost all the while, he would be thinking of how to plan his future course of action. He thought for a few days and was framing his future course of action. However, he wanted to check with his sons one last time before he could decide something.

Diwali was just a month away. In the old days, the three sons would come home during Diwali for a week and spend a good time with the family. But then, it had been a couple of years since they spent Diwali together. Bhaiji, therefore, called his sons and asked them to come home with their families this Diwali. Sumadevi was all excited to see her sons and grandchildren. The haveli was to turn into a home, filled with people and love. Bhaiji wasn't that optimistic. He wasn't sure if his children were excited to be there for Diwali. But he was sure that even if they visited them, it would just be for a couple of days and not a week.

As Bhaiji expected, his younger son made a last-minute excuse to avoid coming all the way to the village for the festival. The other two sons did visit the village but for a shorter duration. Nevertheless, it was a good family time in Nehar Wali haveli. People, food, and celebrations made it lively.

Bhaiji had planned to probe his sons about their views on the estate and the wealth that he had accumulated all these years. Though he always wanted one of his sons to continue managing this, he was now sure that none of his children were ever interested in coming back to the village. On the other hand, they wanted him to sell all the properties in the village and move to the city next to them. The very next morning after Diwali, the sons left, and the haveli again got a deserted look.

A few weeks passed by, and Bhaiji was back to his routine in the village. Just when things seemed to be getting back on track, a tragedy struck the couple. Sumadevi passed away one night while asleep. Bhaiji was completely shattered. The village was grief-stricken. Bhaiji was now left all alone. After completing the last rites, his elder son forced him to come and stay with him in the city. Bhaiji was reluctant, but a few village elders advised him to join the family, at least for a few days. His trusted employees promised to take care of the haveli and the farms. Bhaiji agreed and joined his son on his way back. For good three months, there was not much news from Bhaiji. And then suddenly this morning, four vehicles filled with people reached the Nehar Wali haveli.

The servants in the haveli woke up to the noise and immediately stepped out to see the three sons and their families. They were thrilled to see all of them. But in a second, there was complete suspense and shock. Bhaiji was not seen... where was he.. how come he didn't join them back in the village. Bhaiji could never be left alone in the city, so something was missing. And then came a shock – the eldest son stepped out of his car with a small kalash or a small copper pot. The kalash contained ashes – Bhaiji had expired a couple of days back, and his son was carrying his ashes in the kalash. The servants didn't want to believe what they heard. News spread in the village in minutes, and the whole village turned up at the haveli.

The village had lost its proud son. The entire village was grieving. Bhaiji got a heart attack a couple of days back, and he died even before he could be rushed to the hospital. The villagers were shocked to hear that. They always knew that his health was deteriorating but didn't want to accept that they had lost him. A few elders in the village were furious that they weren't informed immediately. Some of them wanted to see him one last time. The eldest son explained the situation to the lamenting villagers, and they soon accepted the reality. As a last wish, Bhaiji wanted his ashes to be taken to the haveli and then immersed in the stream next to the haveli. The sons had come to the village to fulfill his last wish now.

After a long time, the haveli had seen all three sons together. Of course, it was an occasion of grief, but the sons' sorrow seemed superficial. Though they were sad, they were also keen to know about the wealth left behind by Bhaiji – the haveli, the farms, other investments, and money. They didn't want to talk about this openly, but all three sons were keen to know what they were eligible for and how much would they get as an inheritance. To know more, the sons had decided to spend some time in the village on the pretext of mourning and find the details for themselves.

After a simple lunch, the sons were sitting in the garden when suddenly they heard a couple of motorcycles approaching the haveli. They saw three people walking into the haveli – two of them were familiar faces from the village, and they were their father's old friends. The third gentleman introduced himself as their father's advocate, and hearing this, the three sons were confused and surprised. Soon after Sumadevi's death, Bhaiji had hired a lawyer to prepare his will to ensure proper and fair distribution to all the stakeholders. The lawyer had visited the family to explain this will. The two village elders were witnesses and 'executors' of the will. The sons were confused and wanted to know more.

Bhaiji had left a will to ensure proper distribution of all the wealth he had accumulated over the years. He also wanted to make sure that his wealth was used for the right purpose and for the betterment of the village. Bhaiji loved his sons, and the first part of the will took care of them. He distributed 50% of his wealth equally amongst his sons. They were anguished that they got only 50% of what they thought was rightfully theirs. However, the lawyer went on to explain the will further. Bhaiji wanted the remaining 50% of his wealth to be used for the betterment of the village and villagers. This included upgrading the current village school with a proper building and adequate facilities. Bhaiji also rewarded his key servants, who were with him all the while, with small pieces of land so that they were not dependent on anyone. He donated a part of his wealth to the village panchayat to build a primary health center in the village. He formed a trust with his name to oversee the farms and take care of the laborers. As he did all through his life, this trust was supposed to ensure that no laborer went hungry even during the worst natural calamities. The lawyer assured that he would get necessary approvals and ensure the execution of the will so that all the stakeholders got what they had been promised.

A sense of mixed feelings prevailed all over the haveli. The three sons were a bit upset that they didn't get their fair share. The servants, on the other hand, were completely surprised and overwhelmed with the love their master had shown. The villagers were happy because they now had a proper school and a hospital. The poor in the village were happy because, like in the past, they were assured that their livelihood was taken care of.

Bhaiji always wanted to live after his death. He wanted his sons to take care of his farms and his legacy. The sons, on the other hand, wanted the legacy and wealth but wanted to avoid the responsibility associated with it. However, they realized their mistake as they settled down. They realized how lonely Bhaiji was during his last days. They were so busy in their life that they willfully avoided their responsibility as sons. On the other hand, the villagers and the loyal servants were always alongside the family and ensured that they did everything they could. Bhaiji, therefore, decided to leave a part of his legacy for them to take it forward.

www.ingramcontent.com/pod-product-compliance
Lightning Source LLC
La Vergne TN
LVHW041214150826
845673LV00001B/398

* 9 7 9 8 8 9 1 8 6 9 6 1 5 *